Wide Acclaim for

FALSE MATCH

by

HENRY BEAN

"Buy this book, if for no other reason than as a hedge against spiritual inflation. For *FALSE MATCH*, unlike most of the fiction of the day, will not lose its value. Literature lasts."

—*Boston Sunday Globe*

"A fine, sensitive, and carefully written first novel."

—*Washington Post Book World*

"Erotic, hard. . . . Obsession is on almost every page. . . . Bean keeps the reader reading, wrapping hurt in hot and cold compresses of sure language."

—*Los Angeles Times*

"Crisply evocative. . . . *FALSE MATCH* rings true, again and again."

—*Philadelphia Inquirer*

"The triumph of *FALSE MATCH* is that Bean has it both ways: His book is both a parody of high-lit romance and a heart-punching good read. . . . Great emotional power."

—*Voice*

D1457353

Most Washington Square Press Books are available at special quantity discounts for bulk purchases for sales promotions, premiums or fund raising. Special books or book excerpts can also be created to fit specific needs.

For details write the office of the Vice President of Special Markets, Pocket Books, 1230 Avenue of the Americas, New York, New York 10020.

FALSE MATCH

HENRY BEAN

WASHINGTON SQUARE PRESS
PUBLISHED BY POCKET BOOKS NEW YORK

This novel is a work of fiction. Names, characters, places and incidents are either the product of the author's imagination or are used fictitiously. Any resemblance to actual events or locales or persons, living or dead, is entirely coincidental.

WSP

A Washington Square Press Publication of
POCKET BOOKS, a division of Simon & Schuster, Inc.
1230 Avenue of the Americas, New York, N.Y. 10020

Copyright © 1982 by Henry Bean
Cover artwork copyright © 1982 Fred Marcellino

Published by arrangement with Poseidon Press,
a Pocket Books Division of Simon & Schuster, Inc.
Library of Congress Catalog Card Number: 81-21096

All rights reserved, including the right to reproduce
this book or portions thereof in any form whatsoever.
For information address Pocket Books, 1230 Avenue
of the Americas, New York, N.Y. 10020

ISBN 0-671-54689-9

First Washington Square Press printing January, 1985

10 9 8 7 6 5 4 3 2 1

WASHINGTON SQUARE PRESS, WSP and colophon are
registered trademarks of Simon & Schuster, Inc.

Printed in the U.S.A.

To Leslie Balog

In writing this book many people helped me in many ways. Above all, Leora Barish, David Milch and Ann Patty gave advice and encouragement without which I never could have finished.

But to retell the good discovered there,
I'll also tell the other things I saw.

—DANTE, *The Inferno*

August 12, 1970

I was afraid again this morning. Even before I was fully awake I sensed fear like a presence in the room, and I thought: when I open my eyes it will be right in front of me, a gray figure on the windowsill. Yet when I looked there was nothing there. Above my toes three parallel wires stretched across a white sky, a sea of black roofs receded into the distance, a frame surrounded the window, walls enclosed the frame, the floor came toward the bed, the blanket up under my chin, and the morning said, Yes?, it said, And you? . . . That is a peculiarity of the mornings here in Berkeley, they interrogate.

I sat at the window. I could hear Jimmy and Donna talking in the kitchen. Shaw would still be asleep. Across the street the brown house opened and out came the Portuguese family: man, woman, boy. They climbed into their red Simca wagon and drove off. A moment later Jimmy Wax appeared from our house, got in my Dodge and left for his job in San Francisco. I thought . . . no, it is too simple to say, "I thought." I had ideas, but I also had other ideas. Since I quit my job it is often like that.

I ate breakfast with Donna, read the paper, then went out on the porch for a minute. The Simca was back in its garage, and the Portuguese woman had begun her daily watering of the lawn and garden. She is in her thirties, wears pants, her black hair is stiff and melancholy. Infidelity would become her, but for the same reasons she would never consider it. Above her head a black bird detached itself from one of the wires and flew across the sky, disappearing a second later against the black roofs. It was time to work.

13th

Work: I sit down here at about nine each morning and write for three hours. During that time I am not permitted to daydream, stare out the window, write letters, masturbate, read or make superfluous trips to the bathroom (one an hour is the limit). Occasionally I violate each of these rules, but not often.

Recently I have begun work on a large and still formless project, which I like to think of as a scientific rather than an artistic or literary effort. I am writing this "for myself," as they say, though not without the usual dreams of glory. I once read about a man who wrote in a similar way; a literary agent of some sort would appear in his room at regular intervals and pay him by the pound for his work. Unfortunately the agent is lacking in my situation; no one comes, no one pays, no one reads. I work in a closet, as it were, though not entirely by choice. Twice I have told my roommates that on such and such a corner of this desk was a stack of pages their opinions of which I would be interested to know. As far as I can determine (and I have been scrupulous in my search for evidence), the pages have never been moved. Once I found several scattered across the floor, but experiments proved that they had blown off in the breeze that comes through a crack in the window. In the end I became convinced that none of them had read a word. When I mentioned this at dinner one night, there was silence, which I took for an admission.

More troubling than the obscurity of my labors, however, is an undisciplined quality in the work itself. Despite my efforts, the thing grows in size without any refinement of shape or purpose. The problem is that I cannot resist throwing into it every odd remark and event that catches my attention even for a moment. Just yesterday, for example, I overheard Jimmy Wax on the phone with Lucy. They were arguing about something (a quasi-lovers' quasi-quarrel; Jimmy losing as usual), and finally he said, ''Well, she's mad about him, isn't she? At least in the physical sense . . .''

Now written out here these words look quite ordinary, yet when Jimmy said them they gave me a peculiar shudder. The very flesh of the word ''physical'' (the rough texture of the opening consonants sliding through the narrow vowel to the fricative surface of the *s,* and from there through the second vowel, narrower still, until the whole word bursts into the calm pool of the final syllable) seemed for a moment the purest expression I had ever heard of a love that was indistinguishable from sexual desire. I felt myself grow hot and tight. I wanted someone, but for what?

These sensations occupied only an instant, of course, and my first thought was: how could I use this phrase in my work? It wasn't enough simply to hear it spoken (in fact, that was useless), I wanted to make it mine.

I went to the desk and copied it out on a piece of paper. Yet even in the act of writing I felt it losing its force. Sitting there in my handwriting, the words seemed empty, banal. I tried to recall Jimmy's nervous inflection, his posture as he sat at the top of the stairs, his usually dolorous beard turned a momentary spade of flame in the evening sunlight. I looked in my book to see what I'd been reading at that moment. But the magic of the words eluded me, hovered briefly just a thought away, then receded into the irretrievable distance until I found myself staring at a sentence that, like an exhausted love affair, embarrassed me with the memory of what it had once been.

I describe all this to show how my concentration is squandered in attempts to seize for myself (for my work) whatever glitters out there, gold indistinguishable from the rest. And as a result the work assumes no direction, becomes merely a trash heap of these mental spasms.

August 16

For three years I held a respectable job, one my various alumni magazines could have mentioned without embarrassment. I was industrious, reliable, a productive citizen. People on the street would occasionally say, "There goes . . ." In exchange for my labor I received Blue Cross group coverage, eighty percent of dental work and more money than I needed; enough, that is, to support Shaw and Jimmy as well as myself. So I thought, all right, you've given up the old life, started pulling your oar instead of your meat, and the fear has left you alone.

Then one morning last spring, as if I'd recognized a car

parked across the street, I knew the fear was back. It showed up at work and asked around. It came over to me and said, I know you. So I quit the job and went home. I went home and got in bed, and now when I wake, the gray Berkeley mornings are suffused with fear. Already I am twenty-six.

16th again

All right, perhaps there was something else in my reaction to that remark of Jimmy's the other day, an irritation or annoyance that I failed to mention at the time. Sometimes I do not like hearing about a woman's passion for another man. I can't help taking it as a rejection. Of course this is absurd; the woman (whoever she is) may never have met me, probably hasn't even heard my name. Nevertheless, I find myself wondering what she sees in this man she's mad about and whether she'd see it still after she'd met other people.

Forget this.

18th

I was at the bank today cashing my unemployment check when who should appear behind me in line but Mickey Marcus. Or, as he put it when I greeted him, "Not Mickey, Morton."

I said, "Who's Morton?"

He said, "I am, it's my real name. I'm using that now. Okay?"

"How about Mort?"

He smiled, "If that makes you comfortable."

Mickey brought me up to date with not only some genuinely charming stories about baby Noah and Pamela's complaint that I haven't been up to see them lately, but also the sensational news that he had just sold a piece to *Penthouse*. And for some reason this information did not stiletto my liver as I would have imagined. Growth, I supposed, maturity. I said, "That's terrific, Mickey."

"Morton."

"Morton, that's terrific."

He agreed that it was and then, in an effort to spread the good fortune around, said that Ab Potter ("You remember Ab." "The junkie?" "Not anymore.") had been made *Penthouse's* San Francisco editor and was looking for writers in the area. Maybe I ought to send him something.

"Like what?"

"Whatever you've got and can slant their way." He had done an article on radical sex, how politics could change what went on in bed for certain kinds of people.

"Like who?" I asked him.

He laughed. "Who do you think, man? Us."

Strange, I hadn't noticed. Things always seem the same. For instance, a moment later at the teller's window, Janet said she was about to go to lunch and did I want to go with her? And though it was true that I had come to the bank chiefly to see her, face to face with the invitation I equivocated.

I said, "You're too tall, Janet."

"No, I'm not. We stand on these little platforms." She glanced at her feet. "They're supposed to cut down on robberies."

I tried to see over the counter, but it was too wide.

Mickey said, "I'll take you to lunch, Janet."

She said, "What about your wife, Mr. Marcus, Pamela A.?"

"Pamela A. is okay," said Mickey. "I'm talking about lunch, not bigamy."

But Janet said, "Sorry," and would not talk about either. She also seemed slightly disgusted with me. When she cashed my check, she counted out the money, placing it precisely in the threshold of the window, then withdrew her hands a discreet distance, putting one on top of the other as if to keep them from doing anything wrong. Her fingers were strikingly pale against the dark marble counter. I turned to see if Mickey thought this was strange, but he wasn't watching, and when I looked back there no longer seemed anything unusual about it.

Out on the street, Mickey wrote down Ab Potter's number, and I put it in my wallet. He said, "You know, you could get that style down pretty easily, and once they start buying your stuff . . ."

"Yeah . . ."

"It's good bread, too."

"What?"

"Eight for the first piece, then up a hundred each time."

I said, "What's a piece, Mickey?"

"A piece of what, you mean? I don't know, buddy, that's up to you. I'm just making a suggestion."

Meaning I was a schmuck. I said, "I appreciate it. I'll see what I've got around."

He smiled, "Good," touched my arm and was off to the city.

———

Imagine someone who, in an excess of fantasy, decides to have an affair with a woman he has never met, whose very existence he discovers only by chance. Obviously he is something of an anachronism.

The woman is not his type. She is too tall, too young, too cheerful, too frank. Yet he is a man who does not know his type, or, to be honest, refuses to know it. He is as much offended by the woman as attracted to her. He has fantasies of degrading and humiliating her. He pictures a brief affair that begins with her feeling whole, solid, full and ends when her life and character lie in ruins. It should last two or three months. He would give up other women for the duration. She would arrive about four in the afternoon and leave by six to make dinner for her husband. He would force her to have pleasure. She would be lost.

When I asked Jimmy, he didn't remember the phrase or the conversation. What else had he said? I'd only heard those words. He couldn't imagine who he'd been talking about. He gave me his sly look, "Why do you want to know?"

"Just curious." I glanced at Shaw.

"Come on . . ." Jimmy said with a smile, "I know when something's up."

I said, "Find out who it was, and I'll tell you."

Shaw laughed. Jimmy indicated Shaw, "Does he know?"

I said, "Jimmy, you'll be the very first."

He grinned, "That's the way I like it."

"You were talking to Lucy, maybe she'd remember."

"I doubt it."

"Why not?" said Shaw, "She remembers everything else."

He looked at Shaw. What did that mean? He said, "I'll ask her," finished his coffee and grabbed his clipboard. He was off to work. When the door closed, Shaw and I both smiled.

August 22

The first time I saw Shaw he was in a pose like the discus thrower's but more extreme, and in his hand instead of a discus was a dark green bottle with a burning rag in its mouth. He should have thrown it right away, but he paused a moment, looked around and saw me watching. He smiled. Then the bottle rose into the ice-colored dawn, returned to earth and burst into flame on the windshield of a U.S. Army Plymouth. Fire splashed across the glass and poured in through the windows. A minute later there was an explosion, and flame gushed out both ends of the car. When I glanced back to where the bottle had come from, Shaw was gone.

He had traveled fast and light in those days, involved in politics that were serious, full time and not at all distracted by the electoral process. He was also married, I eventually learned, one of those political couples who never had a roof or a car or a bed of their own, for whom children were unimaginable since there was hardly time or place to conceive, much less bear, nurse and raise. Their life consisted of borrowed rooms, meetings, mimeograph ink, coffee, gasoline,

Benzedrine, theory, strategy, criticism, self-criticism and, at the end of the night, Mexican food and beer. There was also a big, faded purple Indian motorcycle that they both drove.

The only time I met Greta she was so fierce and implacable that even Shaw appeared sentimental by comparison. Their life had a function to which all else was subordinated, and a discipline that must have fed secret appetites. Instead of ropes and riding crops, perhaps, they competed to see who would sacrifice what the other could not, a calculus whose limit both must have seen coming, yet which neither chose to avoid. In the end who left whom? Maybe one night neither came back to wherever they were sleeping, and each, finding himself capable of doing without that, too, stayed away for weeks before learning that the other was also gone.

In any event, Greta took the motorcycle. Shaw heard that she had gone to Los Angeles and become involved in a group with PLO connections; later she disappeared. He did not expect to see her again. One day I met him on the street, and he asked if I knew of a place to stay. Jimmy and I had just rented this house and were looking for roommates. Shaw brought over his few things that afternoon.

In the year since, he has done almost nothing. Days he passes on the Avenue drinking coffee with a few former political friends; nights he reads long, dense texts of political and aesthetic theory, the syllabus of a graduate program he dropped out of three years ago. He sleeps very little. He isn't especially interested in women. When people talk about politics, Shaw rarely participates, or he will say something so oblique and impenetrable he seems to be making a joke at his own expense, the arcane syntax presumably an ironic comment on his current extreme passivity.

One evening last April, Shaw picked up Donna in the

Caffe Med. She thought he was picking her up anyway. She'd gotten into a conversation he was having with some other people, Shaw had mentioned his dissertation ("Class Origins of the Modern American State," one-quarter completed, moldering in his closet), and Donna had said she'd like to see it. So he brought her back to the house, showed it to her, and they sat up talking until four in the morning. When she finally said she was sleepy, Shaw put her to bed alone on the sun porch.

She has been there ever since. For a while she kept after him. She was great looking and unembarrassed as only nineteen can be, and Shaw liked that, but he wouldn't sleep with her. Jimmy got jealous (though of whom and what it would be interesting to know), so Donna fucked him once, but that was all. After a few weeks it settled down, Jimmy got his editing job, and the three of us became four. Now every morning Jimmy drives off to work, Donna practices piano (rehearsals or gigs at night), Shaw does whatever it is he does, and I come up here to write. We pool our money and take turns cooking.

Tonight I made hamburgers, and, while we ate, Jimmy Wax read us a letter he had gotten today from his mother:

Dear Jimmy,

I'm not quite sure how to answer you, because although we have our wishes (and there's certainly no need to go over them), we respect your judgment and your right to lead your own life. I only wonder if "intuition" is the thing to trust with a decision like this when one's entire future is at stake.

We know that you love movies, "passionately" as you say, and that you have felt most fulfilled working on them. You ask us to support you in this choice, and we certainly want to. If we hesitate, it is only because it has seemed to take you so long to complete your projects. Unless I'm mistaken, you've made only two films in the three years you've been out in California, and both of them quite short. I should think a person would have to work a good bit faster if he wanted to make a go of it in film making. I understand that it's a very competitive field and that a great many talented people want to get into it these days.

I confess that when you applied to medical school last year, we both hoped you might finish what Alan started, but you're right, you haven't any obligation to make up for our disappointments. I do trust at least that your decision is not irrevocable. I know you said it was, but so much that we think is final turns out to be anything but. Just to be safe, Dad called the admissions office, and Dick Wheeler assured him they would hold a place for you in next fall's class.

I suppose my real fear is that a lot of intelligent young men like yourself decide in their twenties that they are "totally committed to film," and wake up one morning to find themselves forty years old and living in a rented room. Perhaps there comes a time when we have to look life square in the eye and make hard decisions.

Much love,
Mother

P.S. We're delighted to hear about Lucy, and if she makes you half as happy as you say, she must be really special.

There followed a silence broken only by the faint ping of Shaw's cigarette tapping against the edge of his plate. Jimmy refolded the letter and put it in his pocket. He smiled at Shaw. "You like that?"

Shaw made a noncommittal gesture with the cigarette. Donna went into the kitchen and lit the burner under the coffee. One could feel it happen, the maneuvering around this widening hole. There was something Jimmy wanted from us, but God knew what. Say it was all right, maybe. It's all right, Jim, forget the bitch. Yet Jimmy just kept grinning as if the whole thing were a riot.

Shaw looked at me and raised his eyebrows.

Jimmy said, ''What?''

Shaw shook his head.

''No, come on, what?''

Shaw smiled in astonishment: what was he talking about?

Jimmy waited for an answer while Shaw's smile curled outward at an infinitesimal rate. Finally he said a very quiet and direct, ''Well, fuck you, man,'' got up and left the room.

Donna looked out from the kitchen and said, ''What's with him?''

Shaw made another face: what did she think? She brought the coffee pot to the table and filled three cups. Shaw went into the kitchen for milk, and she called to him, ''Get the milk,'' just as he was coming back through the door with it.

Donna did not like these scenes. Every so often one of us would be seized by a fit of despair over his prospects in life, and Donna would gawk as if she had no idea what the trouble was. Jimmy, for instance, what was his problem? He had a job editing a film ($400 a week and we were living like gentry), he had a new girlfriend, and if he had not quite gotten it completely together yet, he was at least collecting it all in one place. He could be anything he wanted this time around, Donna thought, and she did not like it when Shaw told her that that was not exactly true, that one's mother could set certain limits. . . .

''So big, fucking deal,'' Donna said. ''My Mom's a cunt, too. I don't give a shit.''

Though of course she did. Every time her fingers couldn't forget the years of classical piano and just improvise, Donna would feel her mother watching her practice, that fierce, handsome, stone-slab face yielding not a flicker of approval until Donna had gotten it right, right, right, every note, and who gave a shit for feeling. Donna never mentioned this, but we all heard it when she couldn't play and smashed the keys instead.

Shaw was trying to make her see that, saying, "Donna, listen . . ." But she wouldn't. He was talking about mothers or capitalism or technology (a different trip every night), and she was afraid that if she paid attention it would touch her life, she'd be sucked down into it and drowned. But standing back and refusing to listen, she knew that Shaw was wrong, at least for her. She was nineteen, you made your own, and hers was different.

She got up. He was still talking (softly, it seemed, she wasn't sure), and she interrupted, "Look, I've got rehearsal. Let's talk about it later." Shaw could not believe this. She went upstairs to get her stuff, but his impenetrable surface had been torn open, and she heard him back at the table screaming after her. Donna didn't understand that he wasn't trying to drown her, only show her his own predicament. His and hers and Jimmy's and mine; they were all one to Shaw.

Donna came back into the dining room with her music, but by then he had turned silent as ice. She put on her leather jacket, shook out her American hair. Jimmy was at the table again, drinking her coffee and reading the paper. Donna made a helpless gesture of apology, but Shaw would have none of it. Older brothers had bullied Donna as a kid, and now she had an edge much harder than necessary that was forever cutting things by accident. She felt bad about it, said, "You know I love you guys, but Jesus Christ . . ."

"You love him more," said Jimmy.

She laughed, relieved, but as Shaw's face did not alter, she finally just said, "Okay," and left.

Another silence. Ashes stuck in the grease on Shaw's plate, fluttered like water reeds in the breeze from the door. The sense of an ending. Now what? Then what? Rented rooms.

We adjourned to the living room and watched television, or, rather, watched and commented, our remarks sprinkled through the scenes like supplementary dialogue. We liked talking this way, at and about something external, the TV screen. When we spoke directly to each other, the immediacy inhibited us, we became clumsy, self-conscious and eventually fell silent. The television cured this, unstopped our speech and drew to itself remarks that were, at once, a conversation among the three of us and commentary on its passing text.

At the end of the night there was a film we had watched often, and I began to think (as we responded again to those moments we liked best) that what we share after all these years are the movies we have seen together and that we have agreed to love them instead of each other. Which is to say that I cannot love Jimmy or Shaw, nor can they love me, but that we may all feel for certain films of Don Siegel an affection far in excess of what they deserve. They have become like a trust into which our mutual love is invested and from which a small income is occasionally paid. It isn't a wholly satisfactory arrangement, but it is our own.

Donna came home about two with a guy from her band. She said, "This is Jerry," and we each took an eye from the screen long enough to tell him our names, but then blood was dripping on a black shoe, and we had to look back. The band was all black except for Donna, and Jerry was light black with very black clothes and a black music case in his hand. He stood watching the show because Donna did, and he waited on her word. After a minute she said, "Let's go up," and they went.

We hardly noticed. Lee Marvin had suddenly doubled over, and blood was coming through his shirt, but when the woman moved he mastered the pain and put the gun back on her. She said, No, wait . . . But he couldn't. Lady please, he said, I haven't got the time. A shot. Lee staggered out the front door holding the briefcase over his wound, but it was true, he didn't have the time. Halfway to the car his knees gave, he crumpled, died, and when the briefcase broke open, waves of gray money blew across the lawn. Pull back. End titles. Shaw turned it off.

And now, instead of going to sleep, we drifted out to the kitchen where the strange ritual of separating for the night was indefinitely postponed. We made toast, drank more coffee, glanced at each other furtively. Often it was difficult to understand why we were not going to bed together. When there was nothing left to occupy us, we went upstairs and reconvened at the bathroom door. More talk and amusement but finally each of us went into his room, shut his door, opened his book. Later, one by one, we turned out our lights and jerked off into our towels. I had been abstaining recently, but tonight permitted myself a leisurely session to the tune of this woman Jimmy cannot remember, yet who, like the angel she is, sang me to my sleep.

———————

23rd

Her name is Charlotte Cobin, Lucy remembered right away. Or, rather, her name is Charlotte, Cobin is his, Joshua Cobin; he's in Lucy's class at medical school. What were they like? Jimmy shrugged. Okay, he said, straight, but nice, but nothing special. He only knew them slightly.

"Then how do you know they're so physical?"

"You can tell these things," said Jimmy, "vibes . . ."

Shaw said, "Isn't Joshua the one Lucy's always talking about?"

Jimmy considered this. "Not that much."

"He's a big guy . . . ?"

"Yeah, he was all-coast rugby something at UC Santa Barbara."

I said, "Is he blond?"

"Bronze."

"Jewish?"

"Cobin?" said Jimmy Wax, "Bien tsuris. But he could pass. There're many, many shekels between him and the shtetl."

I said, "While Charlotte isn't rich, but she's more cultured . . ."

He nodded, "Not bad."

"Joshua even seems a little coarse next to her. But they both like that. She thinks he's a hunk, and he . . ."

"He thinks she's sweet," said Shaw.

I smiled. "So how long do you give it, Jim?"

"Give what?"

"The marriage."

"A long time. They're happy."

"They only seem happy."

Jimmy said, "They seem very happy."

"That's always the first sign," I said, "isn't it?"

Shaw laughed.

"Forget it," said Jimmy.

I said, "How does Charlotte pass the time?"

"I don't know. What do you mean?"

"I bet they have a nice place, something in Noe Valley or . . ."

"Diamond Heights," said Jimmy.

"Perfect. You been there?"

"Once. It's nice, but—"

"And they dress well, too. Not just neat and clean. I bet they buy from places you and I never go into. I bet, Jimmy, you've thought about how nice they dress and wondered if you ought to dress like that, too."

Jimmy looked from me to Shaw and said, "So what?"

I said, "They're finished."

"She's yours already," said Shaw.

Jimmy didn't want to argue about it. He held up a roach and asked, "Who wants the rest of this?" No one did, so he took a drag and popped the rest down his throat. Outside a dog barked. We went to the movies.

25th

There were six Cobins in the San Francisco book, only one Joshua. But what had we here? Listed separately, just two lines above, Cobin, Charlotte, same address and number. Is this an affectation or something more?

I called from the phone booth in the Texaco station. A woman answered. I said, "Hello, could I speak to Harold, please."

She had a fine, alto voice, full of confidence and trust. The last thing she'd have expected was what was happening. She said, "What number do you want?"

I read it off.

"This is it," she said, "but there's no Harold here."

"Too bad. What about you? Are you there?"

She laughed. "More or less."

"What are you doing for lunch?"

"I already ate," she said easily, "and besides. . . ."

"All right, I'm sorry." And I was. I hung up. I wished I hadn't called.

———

Broken bones and broken bottles, Robert Mitchum lies dying, kicked in the gut by a brahma bull. Susan Hayward pushes through the crowd. He ain't gonna make it, lady. Mitchum looks up at her, laughs at his pain and, oh, the irony of it. Hiya, Red, he says. Jeff . . . Guess your husband was right about me being washed up. Hayward buries her face in his chest. He winces. She pulls back. Jeff! He's dead, lady. Eyes dry, she goes back outside where Arthur Kennedy reads Mitchum's death in her face, and they walk off together. Fade. Scattered applause. Lights up.

Jimmy Wax twisted in his seat, stretched, groaned, smiled. He said, "What did you think of that?"

"Well, if it had been me," said Lucy, "I'd have gone off with Robert Mitchum the night before. Then he wouldn't have had to get himself killed over it. Such a waste of a good cowboy."

"What about your marriage?"

"Marriages should be permanent, James, not incessant. Her husband was running around with those rodeodies; she had a right to get someone for herself. There's a latent feminist theme in this: if you don't take Mitchum when you can get him, you might have to spend the rest of your life pretending to love Arthur Kennedy."

Donna said, "She loved them both, didn't she?"

Lucy was born for these conversations. She leaned over the back of the seat and smiled. "Can you love two at once, Donna?"

Donna, who'd been sitting with her right arm over the

back of Shaw's chair, now put her left over the back of mine and said, "I can."

Everyone laughed. Lucy said, "Look, they're locking up, they want us to leave." She put on her coat and led us out to the street. Jimmy suggested coffee and dessert, but Lucy told him, "You go ahead. I have to get home."

"Home?" Jimmy was upset. "You're not staying over?"

"Jimmy . . ." impatient, she'd explained already, " . . . I'm on surgery tomorrow at six."

"Six o'clock in the morning," said Jimmy Wax elegiacally. "Where have all the allnighters gone?"

I said, "Shaw still stays up."

Donna said, "I've got rehearsal now."

"That's because he has no one to answer to," said Lucy, ignoring the intervening remark. "You and Shaw are what's left of the leisure poor, Harold."

Jimmy said, "Harold works."

"Oh, right, I forgot," Lucy said to me, "You're a writer, now. How is that?"

"Leisurely."

We were walking along the sidewalk, and as the group stretched out, I let Jimmy go ahead with Shaw and Donna and kept Lucy behind. Away from the others her manner changed, she became even tolerable. She asked me, "How are your parents?"

"They're okay. You've probably seen them more recently than I have."

"Not since the funeral."

"They miss your mother," I said, "my Mom especially. I don't think she's ever going to get over it."

"Me either." Lucy shrugged. "It's so weird for my Dad. He's with this person twenty-nine years, I mean good or bad, every day for twenty-nine years, and then she's just

31

gone. He gets up in the morning, and she's not there." She shook her head. "I couldn't stand it."

"That's why you don't like Arthur Kennedy."

She laughed. "You're right. At least with Mitchum you know he's going to get pissy some day and split, so you never let yourself feel too comfortable."

I said, "It's interesting you should mention this. The other day Jimmy and I were talking about what sounded like some pretty comfortable friends of yours."

"Oh, right, the Cobins." Lucy smiled. "Jimmy warned me about this. What are you up to, Harold?"

"Tell me about them."

"There isn't much to tell. They're pleasant enough. Not terribly interesting. They have a good marriage, though."

"What makes it good?"

"I don't know. Sex probably. They're kind of marvelous looking if you like Californians."

"And we do, don't we, Lucy?"

She laughed. "They're so much healthier, at least on the outside." Then, remembering something. "Except Charlotte limps a little."

"Really?" Mitchum had limped slightly in the movie, old rodeo injuries. "Is she crippled?"

"Of course not. She sprained her ankle rock climbing last weekend."

"How wholesome."

"On mescaline."

"How shoe. Real mescaline, I hope, buttons, not capsules."

"Don't ask me. I never take the shit anymore."

"So tell me, Lucy, are they monogamous?"

A laugh. "Why are you asking?"

"You know I'm always interested in these things."

"Is that because you're a writer?"

"Partly."

We walked a bit in silence, Lucy's mind seeming to wander, and just as I was about to repeat the question she said, "Basically they are, yes."

"Meaning Joshua parks one from time to time."

She shrugged, "Who doesn't?"

"Charlotte."

"That's probably true, but then Charlotte's something of a primitive, isn't she?"

"No question about it."

"There are times," said Lucy, "when they seem like I used to think my parents were. The only two in the garden, you know what I mean?"

I nodded, "Sure, but then where do Joshua's girlfriends come from?"

She gave a sardonic smile and kept walking.

I said, "Well, they sound great, when can I meet them?"

But Lucy would only titillate, never fulfill. "I'll think about it." But of course she wouldn't. "Here we are," she said, tapping the roof of her car where Jimmy, Donna and Shaw were waiting.

The issue of Lucy staying over was still not satisfactorily resolved, so we let Jimmy ride with her alone, and the three of us walked home down Telegraph Avenue. It was a warm and lovely night, the tree leaves whitened by street lamps buried within their branches, and the wind smelling more of spring than autumn. People squatted along the walls, singly and in groups, each of them threatening to make a Christian of you, a Christian, a cuckold or a corpse. Someone in the shadows of the Caffe Med said, "Hey, give me fifty cents."

Shaw said, "What for?"

"Facing your fears." His friends laughed in the dark.

I gave him a quarter. "It isn't helping."

"You don't know what it'd be like without me. Look,

33

here you go . . ." He affected a blank-eyed mutter, "Columbian, man? Clearlight? Deathlife? Hey, you like that? Come on, another quarter, what do you say?" He flapped his arms and barked like a seal. His friends loved it, but we kept going. "Wait," coming after us, "You want to fuck me, guys? Or you, ma'am? Five bucks a trick. Kisses a dollar. You name it. Come on, assholes, don't be such assholes."

"Fuck off," said Donna.

"No? Really? All right, then here it is, my last offer. For ten bucks you can kill my dog. She's worth twenty." A dog had materialized at the end of a length of clothesline the man was holding.

Shaw said, "We've got our own dog. We'll kill her if we want."

"Yeah, but look, this way you get to kill your dog and have it, too. Hahhah. No good? Okay, gentlemen, what can I say? A pleasant night to you all the same."

September 1

Their house is on a hill in Diamond Heights, a working-class neighborhood where young professionals have been buying places recently. A flight of redwood steps leads from the sidewalk up to the front door, and a garage is set under the slope of the stairs. A Borgwaard Isabella is often home during the day, a year-old, gray VW convertible joins it at night. The Isabella also appears now and then in the Castro Street shopping district. A calico cat hangs around the porch; once it killed a bird who was eating at the feeder. There is a lot of contemporary art in the living room, most of it bad. From the windows there is probably a good view of Candlestick Park and the Bay.

The curtains are usually left open at night, and the lights, seen from the street, (especially about two or three in the morning when one cannot sleep) produce a poignant effect. At first they seem to beckon through the glass, to offer warmth, shelter, whatever it is that light implies. But, if one begins to respond, he realizes immediately that the beckoning is in his imagination and that the lights are mute. One imagines that these may be the circumstances in which mass murderers are conceived.

September 2

An interesting detail: Charlotte was brought up on a small farm in the mountains southwest of San Jose. Her family didn't work the land, merely kept a few animals, had a vegetable garden and an acre of fruit trees. They were not wealthy; when her father died, her mother had to sell the place and move to an apartment in Van Nuys where she had relatives. By then, however, Charlotte was in high school, and the farm would have had its effects on her.

No doubt this is what Lucy meant when she called her a primitive. Girls raised in the country are often solitary and imaginative. They read the wrong books, and the dreamy notions these induce are rarely tested against the world. At the same time, knowing nature far more intimately than society, they develop an innocent but powerful physicality.

Charlotte's first social experiences probably intimidated her. She mistook the sophistication of city girls for sexuality and considered herself prudish or immature. It wasn't until college that she realized men were frightened of her, but aroused as well, and for some time she didn't know what to do with all that power.

And in a circuitous way this may explain Joshua's infidelities. His father is a wealthy real estate developer in Santa Barbara, and his mother is a frustrated and melancholy drinker. The combination would have instilled in the son precisely those doubts about his own grip on reality that would make him scoff at anything the least bit vague or ephemeral. Joshua was first attracted to medicine, I imagine, because it dealt in the only particulars he could think of more concrete than profit and loss.

Naturally, then, he would be drawn to a primitive like Charlotte (the antidote to his crushing rationalism), but just as naturally her effortless sensuality would gradually undermine the very project of his life. Now when he watches her sitting in the sun or listening to music, he realizes that for all her vagueness she knows reality as he never will. A part of him understands that she is a door through which he might reach it, too, but he hasn't the courage for that. So he makes fun of her absentmindedness, belittles her confused ideas, and instead seeks out classmates and candystripers, nurses and lab technicians whose fingernails and stifled cries persuade him for the moment that he really is down there at it and has no farther to go.

And Charlotte, meanwhile, stands in their empty living room in the middle of the day, hesitates and momentarily forgets what she was about to do. The light is behind her, so I cannot make out her features, only the graceful modeling of her arms (revealed by a sleeveless dress), and the real motive behind the hesitation, the doubt Joshua has instilled. Portrait of the primitive socialized and, for the first time, wondering at her own purpose. This is where I come in.

Friday

Every relationship is vulnerable from certain angles and in certain lights. You wait, watch, then for a moment it opens and you can enter her life.

———————

September 6

The horror, gentlemen, is precisely this:
there is no horror.

These words appear on the wall of a small office *Penthouse* has rented for Ab Potter, their Bay Area editor and talent scout. Mickey Marcus knew I'd never call, so he mentioned me to Ab, and Ab rang up and said why didn't we get together and talk about projects. I said fine, but sitting on one of those blazing restaurant patios it turned out the projects were to be of my invention. Mickey had apparently told him I had a lot of great ideas for pieces on the local scene, knowing, of course, that I had absolutely none, but calculating that pride or vanity would inspire me to invent what I was reputed to possess already.

And it did. I thought of one, then a dozen. I would say, "We could do something on . . ." Ab's stoned eyes would smile, he'd say, "Great," and I'd say, "Or better still . . ." and Ab would go, "Sounds terrific," until finally becoming depressed by my performance and certain I'd forgotten everything I'd said (we were both far too nonchalant to take notes), I gestured with my hand at an infinity of other projects too obvious to mention, and Ab nodded that, yes, they too were exactly what he was looking for. Well, I thought, and counted my chickens: fame, fame, fame, money, money, money.

Ab said, "What do you know about this guy Divine?"

"Divine the faggot?"

"A transvestite, isn't he?"

"I'm not sure."

"He's getting a lot of play lately; he might make an interesting article."

I said, "Ab, what about all these other ideas?"

"They're fantastic," said Ab. "It seems like there's a lot of interest in guys like Divine right now."

"Yeah, well, look, maybe Mickey or somebody . . ."

"I was thinking of a 'day in the life' kind of format. All the ordinary things this very weird person does: Divine brushes his teeth, Divine has nothing to wear, Divine calls his agent . . ."

"Warhol."

Ab said, "Well . . ."

"Look, it sounds good, but I'm more interested in, uh, political, cultural . . ."

"You don't think Divine's political?"

"Yeah, sure he is, but . . ." And now speech was utterly deserting me because I could hear Ab inside me answering everything I was going to say before I'd said it. And when I tried to anticipate his objections, I could already imagine him answering me there, until finally, in an effort to acknowledge his entire argument and clear away some space in which to speak, I made his case so thoroughly I convinced myself he was right, I should do a piece on Divine.

Yet Ab seemed to understand my reservations completely. He said, "Yeah, you're right, it isn't your sort of thing."

By now I was suffering acutely. My stomach was a torrent of acid. I had to get serious and grow up. I said, "All right, I'll call him."

"You want to?"

"Yeah," I said, sure, anything, just let me get away from here.

Ab paid for lunch, and as we walked back toward his office, I felt better. It seemed I might actually be able to call Divine, endure a day with him and write it up. It might be interesting. It might be weird. I said, "How much for the article?"

"Money?" said Ab. "Depends on the length. Two-fifty to four is the usual range. So how's the rest of your life? You with anybody these days?"

And unbelievably I said, "I'm starting to see someone in the city."

Then it was like a clock. Ab said, "Who?"

I said, "You don't know her. Her name's Charlotte."

"Charlotte, huh, what's she like?"

"She's like we used to be, Ab."

"How is that?"

"I can't remember."

He laughed and said, "You're a hard-liner, aren't you, Harold?"

And I said, "Yes," because I am.

7th

This afternoon, walking on Castro Street, I saw a woman in the window of a restaurant who looked so much like Charlotte that I went in, bought a cup of coffee and sat down a few tables away. She was alone, reading a book whose title I couldn't see and smoking a cigarette exactly as I'd imagined Charlotte would. Her beauty was so graceful and effortless it almost passed unnoticed. No one tried to pick her up; no one eyed her from across the room. Her privacy was respected.

Twenty minutes later she stood and started for the door, and my God she limped, an infinitesimal disruption, unbearably erotic. I was suddenly overcome with fear of exposure. I averted my face until she'd gone, then followed her up the street, right on 19th, left on Diamond. Outside a tall Victorian apartment building she rang a bell and a moment later was buzzed in. I waited five minutes, then quickly walked the route she would have taken going home. When I reached Charlotte's house (it was only a few blocks away) both the Borgwaard and the VW were in the garage.

It wasn't Charlotte today. I described her to Jimmy, and he just shook his head. Depressing.

8th

He didn't just shake his head. He also said, "Listen," and I knew what was coming, "this is a cute idea, very literary, but it isn't going to happen."

I said nothing.

He said, "You'll never do it, you'll just feel stupid. Why not forget it now?"

It seemed reasonable advice. All night I imagined what a relief it would be if I didn't have to keep pursuing this plan and writing it down. So today I put this notebook in a drawer, got out a clean sheet of paper and rolled it into the typewriter. And then it was impossible: there was nothing else in my head.

Finally I understand what Charlotte has become. Every day countless commonplace occurrences (coffee on the porch after breakfast, opening a new can of tennis balls) are seasoned by her imminent presence, are done in some strange way for her. Of course it isn't Charlotte herself but the possibility of her that gives meaning and purpose to the usual redundancy of events. Each time I go for a walk there is a chance I'll run into her on the street, and though I wouldn't recognize her if I did, that only increases the pleasure. Every woman becomes a potential Charlotte, and invariably I see three or four or five who resemble the person I have imagined. Likewise each moment contains the possibility she is watching me, and this gives to the smallest gesture a significance of which it was painfully empty before.

September 10

Lucy is giving a dinner party Saturday. I'm not invited, but we'll see about that. This evening Donna agreed to help me tune the Dodge Saturday afternoon (i.e., show me how), and I said I'd take her to a movie afterward. We have chosen *The Earrings of Madame de* . . ., which is playing in San Francisco at a theater near Lucy's. It is a masterpiece of romantic tragedy, and one of my favorites, but we may have to miss it because there is going to be a hitch in our plans. I have told Donna that she won't need money, that it's my treat (she never has cash anyway), but I will forget to switch my wallet to the pants I'll wear for working on the car. This oversight won't be discovered until we've nearly reached the theater, and though I expect that Donna will suggest going over to Lucy's and getting money from Jimmy Wax, I'll think of it if she doesn't.

The first time you hear a rattlesnake, they say, you know immediately what it is. Your fear explains the sound to you.

———————

September 13

Lucy did not want to let us in. She opened the door a few inches and said, "This isn't a good time, I'm having a party."

Donna said, "We just want to see Jimmy a minute. What's the big deal?" She pushed on the handle. Lucy affected a worried expression and glanced over her shoulder as if the solution to this might lie back there. Donna looked at me, her mouth said fuck, and I think she might have kicked the door open if Jimmy hadn't passed through the hall just then and caught a glimpse of her.

He was a little drunk and delighted to see us. "¡Compañeros!" he shouted. "¿Qué pasa?" threw open his arms, and the door yielded to this enthusiasm. Under Lucy's baleful gaze, Donna went straight to the point (did he have ten bucks he could give us?), but Jimmy was in no hurry. He put an arm around her shoulder and tried to lead her off toward the kitchen. He wanted her to have a drink, help him with the salad, talk for a minute. She resisted briefly, then laughed, put an arm around his waist and went with him.

Lucy said to me, "She's in there."

"Introduce us."

"I have to go cook. You'll know her."

In the living room, five narrow casement windows looked west over a small park, and the low sun flooding through them crossed the thick rug and climbed waist high up the opposite wall. The light was heavy, almost viscous, and for a moment seemed to hold the room in motionless tableau. It filtered among a half-dozen fourth-year medical students, their boyfriends and wives who stood in clumps of longish hair and leather products; there was a sprinkling of turquoise, no Gallo, one Kenzo blouse, one flat-brim leather cowboy hat, one genuine Panama with a parrot green sash, one pair of sixty dollar Fench jeans and one dozen pair of eyes observing the person who had just come into the room.

There occurred, then, a rare moment of class consciousness. Observing my clothes (still streaked with grease from the Dodge), the guests were not sure what I was doing in the apartment. I might have been a repairman sent by the building superintendent to fix something or other, but if that were the case, why was I standing so rudely in the doorway staring at them? Finally a woman at the far end of the room asked if I would like some wine. I said no in a voice that evidently reassured them, for their eyes turned back to each other, and the conversations resumed.

A woman I hadn't noticed before said my name, but when I looked I realized she was talking not to me, but to a little boy of three or four in brilliant blue overalls. The woman wore a crimson dress and squatted easily beside the boy so that her head was about level with his. He placed a reddened forefinger on her chin and said, "What's this?"

She said, "That's my chin," then touched his nose and asked him, "What's this, Harold?"

"My nose," he cried. They had apparently been at the game for some time, for Harold now searched her body for an unnamed part. Finally he poked at her breast and said, "What's this?"

"That's my breast."

He giggled, "No, it's your bosom." In his mouth, the word *bosom* became two balloons stuck together with static electricity.

The woman smiled. "It's my bosom."

Harold shrieked, poked the breast again and said, "What's this?"

"My bosom," she said, emphasizing the round fuzzy sounds and sending him into another fit of laughter. The exchange was repeated until tears ran down Harold's cheeks, laughter drove him to his knees, and he had difficulty catching sufficient breath to ask the question again. But once he had and had received the expected answer, it was as if hysteria took complete hold of him. His face turned crimson as her dress, he drooled, he lay on the floor shaking in spasms of silent laughter.

The woman was laughing, too, so she didn't notice the look of struggle that gradually replaced the boy's smile. He tried to catch his breath and couldn't. His body convulsed in the effort and began to emit a faint clicking. His red face became tinged with violet. The woman was smiling at someone across the room. I stepped around her, lifted the boy by his armpit and slapped him on the back. He coughed. I slapped again. He choked several times, then began to breathe heavily. I set him on his feet. The woman looked at me.

"He was gagging," I said.

She turned to the boy. Having caught his breath, he was standing very still. When he saw her looking at him, he threw himself into her arms.

I said to him, "Is your name Harold?"

He looked back over his shoulder without answering.

I said, "My name's Harold."

"Harold what?" said the woman.

"Raab," and I said to Harold, "What's your name?"

"Harold Bessemer Graves," he said carefully.

I asked him, "What's her name?"

He said, "Charlotte."

"Charlotte what?"

45

"Charlotte . . . Ibywybidybi."

"Charlotte Cobin," I said.

Charlotte nodded.

"No," said Harold. "Charlotte Ibywybidybi."

Having made sure Harold was all right, Charlotte told him she was going to talk to the other Harold now. Then she leaned over and kissed him on the lips, a kiss which lasted a moment longer than it should have, but was the first time I'd ever watched an adult kiss a child without a part of me recoiling in disgust. When they separated, she smoothed his hair, and the boy trotted off.

Charlotte was still squatting, and now started to stand, but halfway up she lost her balance, cried out and would have fallen if I hadn't caught her arm. Instantly a large man bounded across the room and lifted her into an armchair from which he drove the previous occupant with one furious glance. His show of alarm silenced the room, and everyone watched as he brought a leather ottoman up under Charlotte's left ankle (it was already wrapped in an Ace bandage) and lowered the foot carefully. He said, "How does it feel?"

"Fine," she said, "it's—"

"Flex it."

She rotated the foot in a circle and smiled.

"I told you what would happen if you squatted like that."

"It's all right now."

"Every time that happens, it aggravates the original injury. If the ligament isn't allowed to . . ." He stopped himself, leaned down and kissed her. She said, "Joshua," taking his arm and turning him toward me, "this is the Harold Jimmy Wax is always talking about."

He said, "Oh, yes," nodded a vague recognition and sat on the ottoman beside the injured ankle. There being nowhere else, I perched on the arm of her chair, keeping a careful distance.

We talked, or rather, I asked questions, he answered them, and Charlotte watched. Joshua wasn't stupid, but he wasn't very hip, either. He was one of those gentle giants who evidently began lifting weights at the first whiff of puberty and kept at it straight through until he emerged from adolescence diligent, patient and credulous, a believer in cause and effect (in that order), in short, a medical student. This information was as legible in his body as in his words; his hands were big blunt instruments lying on his thighs like abandoned tools, the fingers . . .

But in my reverie, I had accidentally allowed one of his answers to end without interjecting a new question to keep him going, and Joshua leapt at the opportunity. "Lucy says you're a writer." I nodded. He did remember me. "What do you write?" he asked.

A hideous moment. "I'm writing a mystery," I said, and since that sounded good, added "a mystery about time. Slowness is the killer and speed the detective, but for some reason speed can never catch slowness; it's structured around that paradox."

"It sounds interesting," said Charlotte.

"Yes, I've always thought that the detective genre . . ." Naturally, none of this bore any relation to what I'd been writing, but as I listened to myself talk, I began to like what I was describing much better than the work I'd actually done. And it struck me that in a certain way what I'd written so far really was a mystery about time. That wasn't explicit in its current form, but rewritten with a different emphasis. . . .

"I don't follow," said Joshua.

Charlotte said, "I think he means 'bourgeois' in the sense of . . ." She looked at me for encouragement.

"Exactly," I said, "in the sense of . . ." and I decided to rewrite the whole thing. It would become a mystery in which speed gradually learned to let slowness catch him. ". . . a private eye, . . ." I said and laughed. I felt good. "Also, it will be extremely cold," I was apparently saying, "people will freeze when they read it."

"Why do you want to make it cold?" she asked.

"Want to?" I stood up and went to the windows. "Because I'm too warm." Somehow, everyone in the room was listening, and I heard a man ask what movie I was talking about. The sun had gone down, and in the park, a wall of conical trees was silhouetted black against a pale green sky. I opened the second window from the left, and one-fifth of this view hardened and separated itself from the rest. I said, "Magritte," and Charlotte laughed.

"What?" said Joshua.

"It's like 'The Empire of Light'," she said, "by Magritte."

He shook his head as though laughing at his own ignorance, but, of course, he meant just the opposite, that he was too busy with important things, life and death, to bother about this stuff. And that was where I began to lose it and started pushing the conversation any way it would go. "You see, evening," I said, gesturing at the window, "was invented for the working class, but it turns out the rest of us need it just as much."

Donna came in from the kitchen with Jimmy at that point. Joshua looked up at her and liked what he saw, Charlotte looked at Joshua, Lucy at Charlotte, Jimmy at Lucy, and Joshua said, "But you work, don't you?" He wasn't sure. "Writing? . . ."

"Only until lunch," I said.

The same self-deprecating chuckle, "I was at the hospital two hours ago, and I have to be back by eight tomorrow." A moan of mock pity from another medical student, and Charlotte patted his arm.

I said, "But it's satisfying, isn't it, or rewarding or something?"

"It's the real thing," said Joshua. "And it's hot all the time. You get tired, but never bored, because what's happening there," fixing me with his eye, as they used to say, "is very definitely happening."

"It is, huh? You know that's actually a question I've wondered about, what is happening there. I mean, what would you say it is doctors really do for people?"

A judicious look, lips pursed around this interesting question. "I'd say we do the whole range of things, from telling someone he's a hypochondriac to saving his life."

"Saving it?"

"In extreme situations."

"From what?"

"From death," he said, a little surprised it wasn't obvious.

"Save it from death. Is that 'save' like a soul or like a dollar?"

Joshua laughed, "Like a soul, I guess, but more concrete."

"And briefer, too. Saved souls, I think, are never lost; saved lives always are. Actually, the most you can do with life is prolong it and reduce the pain a little, questionable achievements."

"That depends what your life's like."

"Good point. So 'sustain' or 'repair' would be more accurate than 'save'. The most you're doing, I think, is merchandising time and comfort."

He shrugged, and his attention wandered toward Donna. "It's a matter of words."

"And words are important, aren't they?" Charlotte

stiffened. "If we say 'save' we tend to think of God or money, but if we say 'repair' we think of a technician of some kind, a plumber."

Joshua nodded slowly until he found an answer, "Anyone who uses a technique is a technician. Chagall's a technician in a way."

"Fine. Let's call doctors artists, if they like, I just don't want them for Gods."

He said, "That's fair."

Then what seemed a very long look passed between us, a look that was pure tenth grade, and when Joshua finally left to get himself more wine, I turned and found Charlotte frowning at me. The longer I looked, the darker her look grew until I realized that she was mimicking my expression, so I laughed, and she smiled and she said, "Why did you do that?"

"With Joshua? I don't know. Sorry." I passed a hand over my face wiping the expression blank. "Force of habit. I don't like doctors. It's nothing personal, I don't like anybody." I laughed. "What do you do?"

But her face did not immediately agree to this change of subject. "What about your girlfriend, don't you like her?" She meant Donna.

I said, "She's my friend, but just my friend. That's how I go on liking her. Even so it's hard."

"What do you mean?"

"Well, look, don't you hate your husband?"

"No."

"Come on, if you love him, you have to hate him too; that's the rule."

She laughed, "No, I like him."

"Like him, sure; I like you."

"I thought you didn't like anyone."

"I exaggerated."

50

"But you don't hate me?"

"Not yet, but I don't know you very well either."

She laughed.

"So now you have to answer me."

"About what? What I do?" She shrugged. "I don't know. I cook. I clean. I read . . ." She thought a moment. ". . . I take care of the garden. Sometimes I draw a little. Is that enough?"

"I don't know. Is it?"

"Also we do some speculating in art, and I have to keep up with that. It's really what I do most, go around to the galleries and studios, see what people are doing, follow the prices."

"Do you make money?"

"Sometimes. We have three canvases by a guy who just had a show in London. I think we spent about nine hundred for all three, and in London they were going for six and seven thousand each."

I said, "Jesus, you're rich."

She laughed, not at all embarrassed by my rudeness. "I guess I still think of it as Joshua's. See that?" pointing to a burlap and chrome construction on the wall, "Lucy bought it from an artist we know."

"Erotic, somehow, huh?"

She smiled, pleased with the comment. "So is he."

That was a surprise. Joshua was back on the ottoman, but turned the other way talking to Donna. I said, "Do you two see other people?"

"Sure, what do you mean?"

What was I supposed to mean? I indicated the thing on the wall, "Do you sleep with him?"

"I didn't mean that, no." She pushed her foot against Joshua's hip, and without looking around, he put his hand on it. "I only meant that he's very sensual, as an artist. Lots of people—" She cried out and pulled her foot away. Joshua saw it was the injured ankle, moved his hand up the calf and turned back to Donna. Charlotte said, "You think that's very conventional, don't you?"

"Not necessarily. What do you think?"

An instant of mutual dislike came and went; we were not the same sort of people. "I think it's the only way to stay together," she said, a bit pompously and, hearing herself, added "For us. You sacrifice something, but it's worth it."

I said, "I agree."

She looked at me suspiciously, "But . . ."

"But nothing. You're right, it's the only way, and it is worth it. You can't defend it intellectually, but we don't live by the intellect. And over the years, it seems to me, that kind of thing accumulates a meaning nothing else has."

"That's right," she said, "it does."

Lucy announced dinner, and I said, "But . . ."

"At last," she laughed, "but what?"

"But I wonder why you want me to disagree."

"That's a good question," smiling, "come sit with me at dinner and I'll think of a reason."

"I can't, I wasn't invited. Tell me next time."

"All right. Soon?"

"Soon."

She smiled. Joshua helped her up, and holding his arm she limped off to dinner, leaving me alone with Donna in the living room.

Donna said, "You did all right, huh?"

"Did I?"

"Sure, couldn't you tell?"

"What did you think of him?"

"Good looking, isn't he?"

"Is he?"

"He's got a beautiful body."

"You want to fuck him?"

She laughed, "He's too straight."

"He wants to fuck you."

"But so are you."

"Straight?"

"You're a fucking arrow, man."

"A broken arrow."

She laughed, "Warped, maybe."

Lucy came in from the dining room and said, "There's enough food, if you'd like to stay."

Donna got up and pulled me out of the chair. She said, "Thanks a lot, Lucy, but we've got to catch the second show," then indicating me, "Anyway, he got what he wanted."

September 14

I suppose it is time to say something about sexuality, isn't it? I should say that I am hollow and solitary and frozen. I should say that the sedge has withered from the lake and no birds sing. For months and months now. Something happened a couple of years ago. I'm not sure what. Everyone has his sad story (someone who left or wouldn't leave), and I'm too bored to tell mine. I'm not asking for sympathy.

And I don't mean that there has been no one since. There were three or four or twenty, but each left as unsatisfied as she arrived, though none was less than polite. And when they had finally gone, I found that I was happy to lie with my cock cradled in the curl of my fingers and thumb, an orifice which, whatever it lacked in the thrill of otherness, compensated by knowing well the flesh of its flesh. In fact, I would have accepted that onanism had chosen me if these erections didn't keep reaching out for more than I can give them.

Even on the best of occasions, when I have been attentive to myself and elicited fountains, there is an urge left down in there, and one more tender stroke will bring to the surface a last wave of fluid in which swims an opaque speck, hard and white, like a fragment of petrified semen chipped from interior walls. I want to crack this speck open with a fingernail as if inside I would find *it*. What it? Just it, the irreducible nub of things. But the speck always squirts away, disappears into the folds of the scrotum, and when I have finally tracked it down, ferreted it out and cracked it open, there is nothing there. Still, the urge remains.

Two rules:

1. Never mention Joshua. Never engage in discussions of their marriage. Do not become her confidant; it is a sexless role and easy to fall into.

2. A corollary: if she seeks advice, refuse to give it, even when it bears directly on your own interests. Demand, instead, that she answer her own questions, advise herself.

September 16

Lucy came for dinner and has stayed the night, and I have left my door open so I can listen down the hall, for I suspect that her flesh is as cold as mine. Already the noises crawling out of Jimmy's room have an artificial quality; they begin too quickly and the pitch is all wrong.

Anyway, she was hardly through the door this evening

before she asked how I'd liked Charlotte. Her curiosity told me everything I needed to know, but it is necessary to cultivate Lucy carefully. If I seem too interested, it will wound her vanity; if I am casually lecherous she might become protective of her friend. I said, "I liked her, she's refreshing."

"Yes."

"And very competent."

"Competent?" asked Lucy.

"She seemed to know about a lot of different things," I said, "cooking, art, business . . ."

"House plants," said Lucy, "gardens . . ."

"Camping."

Lucy smiled. "Doesn't everyone?"

I said, "I don't."

She laughed, "Well, you're a limited person, Harold, that's your charm." Lucy's physical ugliness is the mirror of her soul, or the converse.

"Refreshing," I said, "because she isn't like the rest of us."

"She is lovely looking."

"Tell me about Joshua."

"Would you like to know what she said about you?"

"No."

"She thought you were cute and very clever."

"Aren't I?"

"You know how impressionable Californians are. I warned her that that was one of your good moods."

"But she knows how envy makes you petty."

"Forget it, Harold, this isn't your sort of situation. They're basically solid."

"That's precisely my sort of situation, and they're not as solid as you think. Do you know why I like her?"

"Because she has a beautiful body."

"I hardly noticed."

"And she's a gentile."

"Is she?"

"I won't have anything to do with hurting Charlotte."

"It isn't going to hurt," I said. "It'll be good for her."

Lucy said, "Really? I can't imagine you being much good for anyone."

And instead of plunging my thumbs through her eyeballs, I said, "Look, could you bring her over here once to visit? She'd like that."

"Why not call her yourself?"

"I'm a little shy," I said.

Lucy's face flattened a moment, then shrugged, indicating she'd decide later what to do, and I wondered what I would have given as my reason for liking Charlotte: the limp? her kissing the little boy? . . .

Now Lucy is pretending to come. It is a trick she learned from books and movies and has improved with a few convincing touches of her own. Still, it is unmistakably a performance, and a vicious one at that. Nothing crueler than faked climax; hatred implodes, pushes her inward, and Jimmy's real one will isolate her completely. Afterwards she'll be depressed, Jimmy will pretend not to know why, she'll say she doesn't either, and he will think she is hiding something even as he refuses to see what it is.

But if she is really hiding something, where has she put it? The problem with faking is that one obeys aesthetic principles instead of erotic ones, and Lucy realizes too late that she began panting too soon. If she tries to make this last all the way through Jimmy's ejaculation, it will oblige her to simulate the transports of multiple orgasm, and that is beyond both her range and her tolerance for self-loathing. Instead she shifts from rapid gasps to a low and irregular moaning that is easier to sustain. Yet gradually this makes her feel insincere as well as frigid and so ugly she can't stand it. Frigid. She knows that until she says the word out loud, there will be no alternative to faking, but how could she possibly say it to anyone? Not to anyone, ever, even in two years of therapy she never has. Alluded to it only. I am frigid, she says to herself, smiling as she imagines these words addressed to a meeting of Frigidity Anonymous, then pictures the faces of the people who would belong to such an organization, the people she has spent her life not being, and no, she will not, she will not, she will never. She collects these thoughts into a hideous mass, and then, as Jimmy's cock sings its sweet song, pushes them away, pushes hard, cries out once from rage not pleasure (though it will pass for either) and after a moment opens her eyes feeling depressed without quite knowing why. When Jimmy asks, she says she thinks so, she isn't sure, and as it all occurred in a moment, perhaps she really isn't.

And now, with the sort of timing I could never invent, Donna is cranking up in the room next to Lucy. One of the men from the band is with her, Jerry, again, I think, and she is coming like thunder out of China. Christ, she must be a fuck and a half, whatever that means. But we know what it means, don't we? And in the silence they leave, I hear Lucy's and Jimmy's tired voices trying to work it out. The words are inaudible, but the tone is clear: question, answer, question, silence, question repeated, anger, silence, attempted reconciliation. . . . But they cannot resolve it, and instead they are falling asleep in the middle. They haven't the energy to go on, because there is no energy anymore. Energy is the latest ethos because it is almost used up. Good-bye to that one. A page turns in Shaw's room. The world is falling asleep, and so am I, so let's just stop kidding ourselves and turn out the light.

17th

At seven this morning my father called to tell me that his parents were flying to Florida this evening and would I please give them a call around noon. At nine, therefore (noon in Philadelphia), I called and got no answer. I called again at ten and eleven, but still nothing. Around dinner the phone rang, and it was Manny again wanting to know what went wrong. I explained, and it turned out he had meant noon my time. At noon their time they were out to lunch with him. Then he came back with them and waited around all afternoon for my call. Why didn't he call me? He didn't want to spoil the surprise.

He gave me their number in Florida, and I dialed it immediately. The entire conversation lasted ninety seconds because my grandparents, I realized, were even more uncomfortable talking to me than I was talking to them, and they got off the phone as fast as possible. By the time I hung up, I was actually insulted. Then, of course, I decided it was all my fault, that despite my proclaimed politics I oppress my own grandparents with class distinctions.

Sometime next week I will get a note from my father saying that he talked to his parents and that they were delighted by my call. "I can't tell you how much these things mean to them," he will write, and I will know the sense in which that is true.

19th

All the same

As what? I wrote those words twelve hours ago and now can only guess that they were a form of "nevertheless" and not a statement of mysticism or monotony. Anyway, as soon as I wrote them, the phone rang.

It was Lucy, full of coffee, saying, "Good morning, Harold, what are you up to today?"

I said I was working.

"On Saturday? How industrious. Listen, the reason I'm calling is that Charlotte Cobin and I are coming over to Oakland this morning to look at some ceramic work, and we thought you might like tagging along."

"Well, I'd love to see you both, you know . . ."

"Yes, I know."

". . . but, as I said, I'm working now."

"That's too bad."

"So maybe you could drop by early this afternoon."

Silence for a consultation. Voices in the background, Jimmy's and Charlotte's. One of them said, "How about lunch?"

I said, "Lunch is perfect."

"Why don't we meet for lunch," said Lucy. She named a restaurant.

"One thirty?"

"Make it two."

I got there early and sat on the patio drinking a beer. At another table a woman with black hair and a coltish face sat alone under an umbrella, and I thought, why not her instead

59

of Charlotte? Why not both? I felt good. The work had gone better this week, was beginning to move, and lately I had been less preoccupied with failure and rented rooms.

A woman was standing on the flight of steps that led down to the patio, and she gazed out over the tables. She had long hair, her arms were bare except for a black bracelet, and there was a bandage around her ankle. Lucy stood beside her. They waved.

I said, "I didn't recognize you."

"She has her hair down, today."

"It was the ankle."

Charlotte smiled.

"Harold's always had something about injuries, haven't you?"

"Something," I said.

The women looked at each other.

I said, "What did she tell you?"

"Just what you told me once," said Lucy, "that the greatest pleasure was giving pain."

As if one's own memories were not hideous enough. "That was Baudelaire," I said, "not me."

A waitress brought menus, and we ordered three beers. Charlotte smiled at me, "How do you give pain?"

I said, "Do you believe everything Lucy tells you?" I wasn't sure if I meant that seriously or not, but Charlotte just laughed, and I didn't like it. I said, "Is that funny?" She stopped laughing. I said, "Did you ever want to hurt anybody? Just to hurt them?"

She shook her head. "No."

"Then don't joke about it."

Instantly blood filled her face. Irish capillaries. She said, "I'm sorry," glanced angrily at Lucy, "I thought we were just kidding around."

I was embarrassed. I laughed.

"He is," said Lucy, "that was a joke," though she hadn't been sure herself for a moment.

Charlotte looked at me, puzzled. She didn't really believe that.

I smiled, "I thought you knew."

Lucy said, "Pretty funny, huh?"

Charlotte covered her eyes for a moment, then looked up and laughed. "I feel stupid."

"Exactly," said Lucy, "that's how."

The service at the restaurant was slow; beers kept coming, but no food, and the mutual influence of heat and alcohol soon made us drowsy. Silences began to perforate the conversation and I had the sense things were not going well. Why were we here? Charlotte went to the bathroom, and Lucy and I sat opposite each other looking at the salt. Eventually she said, "Making a fool of her didn't help." The woman with the coltish face appeared again, walking toward the steps. Lucy said, "There's Leslie."

"Invite her over."

"Leave her out of this one, Harold. You've got problems enough with Charlotte."

"Like what?"

"I don't think she likes your type."

"What type is that?"

She looked to see if Charlotte were coming back. "My brother used to say something about playing basketball with you. You couldn't shoot, wasn't that it? 'Harold's got all the moves,' he'd say, 'but the ball just won't go in for him.' I thought that was perfect."

"What do I do to you, Lucy?"

No response.

"Why did you bring her over?"

"Just to watch."

"You'd like to see them split up, wouldn't you?"

"What for? I'm not interested in him."

"Who said you were?"

"Jimmy and now you. That's probably where he got it."

"No, I knew you never would be. I think you just like people splitting up."

She laughed, "You're such a romantic, Harold, no one's into that kind of thing anymore except you."

Charlotte returned and lowered herself into the chair with a hand on my forearm. Then I got up and on my way to the toilet asked the waitress where our food was. She said it was coming. She was a pretty woman, but seemed sick of seeing her looks in customers' faces. Last year she'd worked at a cheaper place down the Avenue; tips were better here, but someone had told me the waitresses had to fuck the owner or manager or someone.

It was heavy piss, cider colored from the hole, then sparkling gold for a few inches where the arc crossed a shaft of sunlight, and dark again as it fell into the bowl. The light made the stall seem a tiny church, and I thought, Christ, did I love drinking and pissing and pissing drunk, it was the closest I ever came to prayer. Saturated, all sensation balanced, the body reached a nil point, and then there was just thought swaying above a drunken piss like a man on a pole.

At the table, the food had arrived, and they were busily eating. I wasn't hungry, anymore, but made a show of enjoying it, not wishing to criticize the restaurant they had chosen. The meal was now diffuse and without focus; it hurried to be over. The afternoon had been a mistake for which each of us felt responsible.

"We should go soon," Lucy said when she'd finished. "Joshua's off at five today."

I said, "Let's have one more round."

She said, "I don't need it; I'm sticking to the chair as it is."

"No one needs it, Lucy, but summer's over, and we ought to have a last beer, just to say good-bye to it, okay?"

She said, "It's not the end of your summer. You do what you please."

"Oh, Lucy, you just don't get it, do you?" I caught the waitress's eye and pointed to our empties. Lucy looked away, and I knew that if I let myself think about her I'd get depressed. I said, "Lucy, come on, relax for ten minutes and have another beer."

She said, "Look, don't pull that earthy shit with me, I've heard it before. Drink all the fucking beer you want, but don't tell me to relax, all right?" Her face was a tomato. She said, "Charlotte I'd like to go."

Charlotte didn't know what to do. The waitress put down three cold bottles and took away the others. I filled everyone's glass and said, "To Lucy."

Lucy said, "Shut up," loud enough to turn heads, then repeated it softly, almost to herself, as if that would muffle the first. "All the uptight, little Jewish men," she said, "they come out to California after college, get laid a couple times, take some drugs, and the next thing you know there's a plague of scraggly beards running around spouting this hippie shit about have another beer and relax, assholes who never relaxed ten minutes in their fucking lives. Harold, do you have any idea how stupid you are?"

"I don't have a beard."

"No? Well, you might as well. It seems like it's there anyway, a beard, tefillin and a nice black yarmulke with the bobby pins." She laughed and looked at Charlotte. "You know what tefillin are?"

Charlotte shook her head.

"My first boyfriend was like that," Lucy said, "one of those sadistic Jewish geniuses. He kept telling me I was too thin and too rational. He said, 'Put on some weight. You're too abstract, drop a little acid; you're uptight, I'm going to have to fuck your ass.' He said I couldn't come because I was a Nazi, but he'd teach me. He said he knew a lot about sexuality. He said, 'You've got to break it down. Everything. Smash the psychic state.'

"So, I thought, okay: I ate until I was sick. I took drugs, Jesus, you wouldn't believe the shit we took, stuff my pharmacology professor never dreamed of, and I'd go to work every day while he stayed home reading Mallarmé and teaching himself Chinese. I'd say, 'I want to learn Chinese, too.' He'd say, 'Fine, quit your job.' I'd say, 'Are you going to work? ' 'No.' 'Then we'll starve.' 'We won't starve.' I'd say, 'Look, I can't live like that,' and he'd say, 'That's your problem. I can.'

"We'd fuck whenever he said, morning, night, or never if he didn't feel like it. Sometimes he'd call the office and I'd have to come home for lunch so he could fuck me then. I got fat. He said, 'You're ugly, it makes me sick, I can't get turned on to you.' I said, 'You told me to eat.' 'You overdid it.' So I dieted, but I couldn't lose the weight. I started thinking I was crazy. I told him the drugs were fucking me up, but he said I was finally letting go, and it was scaring me. I couldn't remember things. I'd space out in the middle of sex, work, driving the car. I hated fucking. If I wasn't lubricated, he'd scream at me for holding out on him, then he'd shove it in dry because Vaseline was a crutch. 'Technofuck.' He wouldn't do it. We'd be in the middle, and he'd say, 'What's wrong?' I'd say, 'Nothing. It's great.' 'Then what's wrong? ' 'Huh?' He'd say, 'What is it with you? Why can't you do it? You're hopeless you're so fucking frigid.' I thought I was going to have to die to fix what was wrong."

She blew into the foam of her beer and took a sip. She'd had no trouble saying frigid. "So spare me the advice, Harold, I don't need it anymore." She put down the glass and stood up.

Charlotte didn't move, just sat staring at her plate a long time, then finally wiped her face with the napkin. She and I walked out onto the street together while Lucy went to the bathroom. I said, "I'll call you." She nodded, and I said, "Is that all right?"

"I don't know." She began to cry, and I wanted to tell her not to, to explain that her expression back at the table, just short of tears, had been perfect, but that this went too far. She should have left this implied. A couple passed and stared at us.

Lucy said, "Let me drive." Charlotte gave her the keys and got in the passenger door.

I said, "See you Lucy."

She said, "Eat shit," and went around to the other side.

Charlotte rolled down the window and I kissed her. I said, "We'll talk." She nodded. They drove away, and I worried that the kiss might have seemed perfunctory, a convention of the genre. Had she felt its insincerity? It wasn't really insincere, merely calculated. Did she understand that it was impossible not to calculate, that calculation was a refuge for awkwardness? Jimmy Wax once made a hundred dollars by spending a weekend in Stanford Hospital with a tube down his throat, another up his rectum, and a cleaning solution running through him until it came out the bottom as clear as it had gone in the top. Then he was like a new baby inside, immaculate from mouth to anus.

Standing alone on the street I felt much drunker than I'd been at the table. Maybe it was the heat and the sweat as well as all the beers. It was kind of trippy in a way. The air seemed singed like burnt paper, and I was struck by the beauty of the women and the beauty of the men. Even the youngest had acquired this afternoon a gold patina, a color not dissimilar to that of my piss in the sunlight, and as everything was slowly enameled in this glow, it became ever more beautiful. A woman at the corner turned, and the gold spilled in streams from her lips and shoulders, shook in showers from her hair, and even as it fell away, she became golder still; her red hair was gold, her gray eyes were gold, gold was in the hollow of her throat and trailed like dust from her fingers. She seemed a god incarnated right here on Telegraph and Channing. Then she laughed gold, and became a man, I realized, or perhaps he was another, fat and black, and there was another still, green gold, Quetzalcoatl walking up Dwight Way, stepping in and out of the sunlight.

I said to Shaw, who had been walking at my side for some time, appearing from Quetzalcoatl knew where, "Look at them, they're all gold."

He looked and said, "What do you mean?"

I wasn't sure. I thought: don't ask, just be my friend and know. For as I tried to formulate an answer, the perception faded, the gold became brass, the brass butter, the butter a light in the last summer sky and no longer an attribute of the earth. So I shook my head, I meant nothing, and we walked on together, pals who could not talk. Who could talk quite easily, rather, for in fact I was carrying on a perfectly lucid conversation, telling him everything that had happened at lunch, while I was also silent and alone.

He said, "Let's get some coffee."

I said, "Okay, where?" and he motioned like a magician who had just produced on our left the patio of The Boat where an empty table waited at the edge of the sidewalk. I sat in the shade of a listless tree while Shaw went inside to get the coffee. Across the street, a sign on a twenty-foot pole said TEXACO, then turned around as if to show something else on the other side, but this, too, said, TEXACO. A woman with honey hair and nail polish rode up on a bicycle.

She pushed a pair of sunglasses up on her forehead, looked around and asked if I was Leo Hummel. I said no. She said damn, this was the third time she'd tried to meet him for lunch. Lunch? it was almost five o'clock. Ah, that explained it; well, would I like to have lunch with her? Sorry, I'd eaten. Dinner? Not yet, but if she waited . . .

She shook her head. "I'm famished now. Anyway, I'm not liked here." We both glanced around.

"Why not?"

She studied me warily and raised her eyebrows. "I'll tell you another time. Call me at the animal labs in the Tolman subbasement. Imogene." She extended her hand.

I said, "Harold," and we shook.

"Don't forget, Harold."

"I remember everything."

"Really? You must be paranoid." She mocked a knowing smile, pushed the glasses down onto her nose and pedaled off.

"Who was she?" said Shaw, appearing with two coffees.

"Imogene. Like her?"

"I didn't say that."

"She's a minor Aztec death goddess."

"You think she'd kill me?" said Shaw.

It was the funniest thing anyone could have said. My sides hurt, and my nose ran as we stood on the curb waiting for a break in the traffic. The old happy hopelessness, it made the world right. A giant red bull's-eye sat on the housetops across the street, and I was slimy with various fluids. The days were getting shorter, and the truth was I loved it all, the things I complained about and the complaining and even the agony, whether real or not. How could I not love it?

Shaw said, "Run," and I tried to follow but my feet were numb. It was like running on artificial legs, and I wondered how many times I had stood on curbs waiting to run for the other side, a thousand different curbs and other sides. But all the same, they were all the same. I stopped in the middle of the street between the white lines, and once I'd begun to look around, lost my sense of which way Shaw had gone or where the restaurant was. A sign turned slowly revealing, letter by letter O C A X E T, and the last letter was Shaw. He stood on the far side leaning at a ridiculous angle against a telephone pole and applauding.

I ran.

Shaw glanced up the street. An avalanche of horns and shrieking rubber crashed over me, and amid this general din I could distinguish the violent engine and black odor of an AC Transit bus. It appeared first in an obscure corner of the periphery, but an instant later half the world had become a wall of glass and welded steel plate coming too fast from too close, and I wondered if Lucy had been right, that dying was the only way to fix it.

Shaw's face floated dead ahead, close enough to kiss, and he reached out for my shirt as I moved forward. The bus flicked my pant cuff. Two white buttons popped into the air, I reached for them, missed, sat down and slid backwards across the sidewalk. I heard Shaw saying that everything was all right, and when I tried to disagree realized he was talking to someone else. The bus and several cars had stopped to see what had happened, and their windows were filled with faces staring at me.

Laughing, Shaw gave me a hand up, and I said, "What time is it?" He didn't know. "Shit, look at my hands." They were scraped blood and imbedded with pebbles. My pants were torn from hip to knee.

"Look at you," said Shaw.

"Christ, look at me."

———

Sunday

My next conversation with Charlotte should occur twice as quickly as the last one, making Wednesday the natural choice. Therefore Tuesday is perfect, so I will call Monday. During the day while he is at work? Not at all. Rule 3. Eschew deviousness. I will wait for tonight's football game. The Rams should take the lead in the first half, and with Kilmer unable to move Washington, Allen will be obliged to open the third quarter with Jurgenson. Sonny will march the Redskins to a quick touchdown and field goal, and early in the fourth he will get the ball again and begin driving for the lead. Charlotte and Joshua went to college in southern California; she may have become a fan through him, but since her interest is derivative, she will be obliged to answer the phone. The noise from the television will cover the conversation, but she won't realize that Joshua hears nothing. She will hurry to get off. She will be sitting beside him again before she has time to think about what has happened.

21st

Jurgenson's first pass was incomplete. The second was intercepted and returned to the Washington two. On the next play, Gabriel faked into the line and rolled around right end: 26-3.

This wasn't my fault, of course. Or was it? One has to accept responsibility for his plans. If they fail, we assume he didn't want them to work out, don't we? That he never really intended to call. That he is a coward as well as a failure. A failure as well as a coward. Unless, of course, he shows some guts and calls anyway.

On the sixth ring Joshua answered with a preoccupied "Yes?" I wanted to hang up right then, but in a moment of panic thought that if I did he would immediately know who had called and why. So, instead, I heard myself go through the formalities of inviting them both to dinner while he muttered something about not knowing "what we have planned for this week," as Charlotte was "out at the moment."

I said, "Really? Where is she?"

A hesitation. "She went to an opening."

"One of your artists?"

He didn't like this, but what could he say? He could say, "Yes," and he did.

"The one who did the thing at Lucy's?"

"Actually, it's a group show at the Eidetic."

Actually? Why actually? "Well, talk it over when she gets home."

"I'll have her call you," he said.

"Do."

So, off dallying at the gallery, was she, while Joshua boned up on anatomy? How would that affect my chances? Did it mean the door was open or that the room was occupied? If she were already into something with the very erotic artist (no reason she should have told me the truth), she'd hardly be interested in the peculiar pleasures I offered. On the other hand, if she dallied not, nor did she linger, she might appreciate the message behind my message and arrange something.

22nd

Rule 4. Never use secondhand information directly. Do not say, "Jimmy tells me you've been in a bad mood," rather, "You seem restless."

23rd

I have a rival and a careless one. Charlotte called this afternoon, apologized for not getting back to me sooner, then asked if I would like to go "with a few of us" to see *It's a Wonderful Life* at one of the revival houses in San Francisco. Now in this choice of film I detect a taste unmistakably foreign to both Charlotte and Joshua. The erotic artist, on the other hand, might like Frank Capra movies; they would let him indulge in sentimentality without any risk to his taste. Yet if he'd thought about it for even a minute he would have realized that this was just the sort of film to send Charlotte running home to Joshua the minute the lights came up.

But what could I do to avert this disaster? If *Duel in the Sun* were playing somewhere, or anything by Sirk. . . . Lacking that, I could go along and try to criticize the movie afterward, but this would only seem to be ruining their fun. I hesitated, stalled, and then, as the very rhythm of my fear reminded me of Brer Rabbit, I realized that bad propaganda could be used as effectively as good.

"It's a Wonderful Life?" I said, "terrific. You ought to go. I just can't watch that stuff anymore."

She'd never heard of such a thing. "Why not?"

"Because I fall for it every time."

"Fall for what?"

"That whole view of life."

"What is it?"

"Go see it and tell me what you think."

I heard her interest silently aroused. She won't recognize that I've spoiled the movie for her; she'll be too busy looking for that whole view of life to notice what's been lost. And if I handle our discussion afterward correctly, this should also deal with the problem of the artist.

September 27

She comes for lunch tomorrow. It pours today.

Last-minute misgivings, thoughts of despicable calculation. Fear of being laughed at. Fear of hurting her. Fear of failure to: (a) seduce (general), (b) seduce (specific), (c) satisfy (general & specific). Thoughts of my own worthlessness intrude and sound the retreat. Get out while you can. And this is half the point, isn't it? To seduce myself as well as her.

September 29

A conversation like the long tacks of a sailboat, moving always away and always back. What is Capra's view of life? When did I stop going to movies like that? What do I think of feminism (she calls it "women's liberation")? Am I a communist? Is romanticism bad? Do I believe in Freud?

And all of these questions, like a spiral of straight lines defining a circle, enclosed another, unasked: who was I? She had just noticed that this odd figure who appeared recently on the periphery of her life was perhaps interesting. She began to hear the things he said, remembered others he'd said a week ago, and now she wondered if he didn't see through it all as she did.

I answered her questions, found that my ideas came fluently and that for once I knew what I thought. I was brilliant. I talked of love, sex, sports, and God, and after one particularly stunning riff (the substance of which I have mercifully forgotten), I realized with a flush of embarrassment that she wasn't listening, or, to be exact, she liked the music, but hadn't really been paying attention to the lyrics. The truth was, Charlotte wanted to talk about herself. But of course, I said, I understand completely, let's talk about you. Only first why don't we get a cup of coffee and go up to my room?

"I really don't know," she said, "I guess I'm a little bored. Josh says I just have to make up my mind."

"About what?"

"What I want to do." She smiled. "His first couple of years in med school I didn't think about it. I read, I . . . but now . . ." But now he is doing clerkships, wears a white coat and sees patients. He works nights, comes home from the hospital and sleeps, gets up and goes back. She has realized he is going to be a doctor, and she is going to be nothing. "I might go back to school."

"In what?"

"History of art? . . ." She shrugged. "Maybe anthro."

"Would you like teaching?"

"I think so. I'd like to feel I really knew something. Of course you never know enough, but . . ."

"You'd like to be paid for what you know."

"That's an interesting way to put it."

"It's the only way."

"Or even psychology. I was good at that in college."

The problem with psychology was that a doctorate took so long, and she didn't know if she wanted to write a dissertation. An MSW depressed her. But there weren't many jobs in art or anthropology.

"Is a job really necessary?" she asked.

I said, "The question is what you want."

"I'd like to be independent."

"Economically?"

"I guess that's a necessary part, isn't it?"

She wanted to see some things I'd written, so I dug out a few pages, random fragments, and she said she liked them. One passage seemed to move her. She was sitting on the edge of the bed, and I was at the desk about eight feet away. I thought about it, but couldn't imagine how to cross that space. Long before I got there, she would see me coming, and I would have to go the rest of the way observed and with my intentions known. Once I had known how to deal with these distances, but no longer. So I saw her out, feeling ridiculous and quite sure she found me so, and put a hand clumsily on her shoulder. Not knowing how to respond she leaned against it and, after an awkward moment, got into the car, and started the engine.

I said, "Come again."

"Maybe Thursday, I'll call you."

We kissed, tenderly now, every ounce of pressure and the slightest movements like negotiations of a contract, offers and tentative acceptances, deposits and conditions, all of which became completely stupid and banal the moment she'd driven away.

Thursday

She said she'd call, and she hasn't. I tell myself something came up, but the fact is she just forgot. Or didn't forget, simply found something better to do and felt no compunction about letting me know.

In the morning I tried to work, but after every couple of sentences found myself expecting the phone to ring as a reward for that small effort. And every time it did not, I felt humiliated for having thought it would. Yet when I tried to picture Charlotte calling me, I couldn't do it. I could see her walking through her house, passing telephones in every room, but I could not make her reach out and lift the receiver. Once I got her to pause and turn as if to call, but then something off-screen distracted her, and she was gone.

At noon I came downstairs and found Shaw slouched in the green chair, throwing a tennis ball around the living room. It hit the ceiling, a wall, bounced on the floor and fell precisely into his hand where it lay open on the arm of the chair. He smiled at this, looked at me. "No word from her?"

I said, "It's over."

He laughed, flicked a three-surface shot in another direction, the ball returning almost to the same spot, Shaw skill-fully disguising the slight movement of his hand this infinitesimal inaccuracy necessitated. He raised his eyebrows in mild self-criticism. "Go for a walk," he said, "don't let her catch you around the house all the time."

I crossed the campus and set out through the north side where the Berkeley that is Berkeley is replaced by pined-and-spruced houses-with-views on roads without sidewalks.

The point was I should have taken her on Monday. Granted all the arguments against that sort of thing, the fears of rejection and failure, the political objections, moral objections, the late hour, the dirty sheets, the unsettled issues of contraception and disease, I still should have. Taken her. I won't want to argue about what the words mean; you take them or you don't. She'd have called today if I had.

October 3

A party last night. I wouldn't have gone, but Jimmy told me Charlotte would be there, so earlier in the day I walked up to the bank and asked Janet what she was doing that night.

We arrived late. Janet wore a long black dress to a party of blue jeans, a dress so heavy with the hours it had cost her at the teller's window that I was instantly depressed and exhausted by the sight of it. Yet it produced exactly the right effect: Charlotte took one look, and her face asked, what in the world is he doing with her? Snob. So the four of us stood chatting for a few minutes while Janet's carnality gradually made its point (one not lost on Joshua), and when I was sure

Charlotte had sufficiently intimidated herself, we said good-bye, and I led Janet out onto the back steps.

"Is she your girlfriend?" Janet asked.

I said, "Who?" We had run into several women I knew.

"The one with the boots."

"Charlotte? She's just a friend of ours. That was her husband."

Janet made a face dismissing husbands. "I didn't know your friends were going to dress like that."

I nodded. "It doesn't matter; no one cares."

"I shouldn't have come," she said.

"Why?" It was true. I kissed her. The dress evoked a college prom, my spartan room, cummerbund and corsage undone, not withdrawing just this once and thinking we could feel it spark and ignite right there, as if the kid who wasn't going farther than a toilet bowl cried out once from its hypothetical future.

Janet said, "Harold."

"What?"

"Let's go back to your house and fuck all night."

Janet was drunk, and on the way home she worried that I was going to be disappointed in her.

"Why would I be disappointed?"

"My body's ugly."

"No, it isn't. Why do you think that?"

"It used to be nice," she said, "but now it's ugly."

"Why? Do you have scars? I like scars."

"Lines," she said, the lines her children had drawn.

I said, "I've seen lines, they're okay."

"I don't want you to be disappointed, Harold."

"Don't be ridiculous."

"I want you to fuck me all night."

"If I can."

"I know you can. I can tell you're great."

But then the bank teller's long white body stretched out on my sheets in the moonlight, and though she was almost too drunk to notice, I was not great. In the beginning was the end (confirming my dislike of mystical unities), and even before I could apologize, Janet was asleep.

Monday

I said, "Listen, Charlotte," I was on the bed this time, she was at my desk, "I want to ask this in a general way because I feel like I need a sense of where things are going and how you're into this."

"This?"

"Us. Sexually. I don't necessarily mean right now, but if you think it's a foreseeable thing or not."

"You mean if we're going to have a physical relationship."

"Right."

"Do you want to?"

"Of course. Yes."

"I wasn't sure."

"Really?" Horror show. "Why not?"

"I don't know. You just didn't seem to."

"I think I'm always a little ambivalent about it. With everyone."

"Why is that?"

"I guess I'm afraid."

"Of me? Women?"

78

"Not exactly; it's complicated."

"But you do want to?"

"Definitely."

"Good, so do I. Can we cover that window?"

Rather, I did want to, and I didn't, and I could not tell which was primary. But at moments like this the wanting usually seemed far away, beyond the fear, and I could not really feel it; I had to push my way forward on faith, knowing there was no choice except to go through sex toward wanting, to keep pushing continually into the present, through whatever I thought or felt, whatever came at my face, just going. I was afraid of the fears ahead, but more afraid of those behind, and the only way to go on was to be willing, indeed to transform myself into a total willingness without aim or object, as if offering myself as a sacrifice to events; it seemed that only the tide of events could carry me past the fear and into my wanting. And if it came to nothing, if in the end it were nothing, again, that had to be all right, for there could be no forcing it, right? The flesh didn't lie. And if the flesh were mute, well, that was okay, it was fine, it was great, at least it was the truth and exactly what I'd expected.

I said, "Don't do that."

"Why not?"

Difficult to say. "Because if I can't do it the right way, then this seems just . . . I don't know."

"Why is that the right way?"

"Yeah, I know how it sounds, but all the same there is a sense in which letting you do that is very passive, isn't it?"

"I don't know."

"See, I feel like I have certain tendencies in that direction that I don't want to encourage. I think if I let myself get into it, I'd never want anything else. Anything."

"So what?"

"You wouldn't care?"

"There are things I like."

"Sure, I know, that's not what I meant. But you wouldn't mind if we just did this?"

"I don't think so."

"Most women would."

"I don't know about most women."

"Actually, neither do I. I don't think I even know about the ones I've known; both, four. Still, don't you think fucking the normal way is really the essence of it?"

"You mean we should be having children?"

"Yeah, maybe. I guess I'm something of a prig, aren't I? But I've always thought that was the pure form, and the rest were just derivations."

"Have you done a lot of experimenting?"

"No." Do I know what I'm talking about? No, I have a feeling. Based on? A feeling. "Have you?"

"A little."

"And?"

"I don't know. The pure form seems to be important to you."

"I don't know why. I used to think that if I didn't allow myself this other stuff, eventually I'd have to get back into fucking. Also, there's a particular kind of intimacy to intercourse."

"But so is there with this?"

"Yeah? You like doing it?"

"A lot. Don't you?"

"Sure."

"Okay, then?" She took the top in her mouth.

"Yes."

She removed it. "I don't want to compromise you."

"For Christ's sake, please compromise me."

That is not to say that she was neglected. When time had

passed and I felt moved by more than reciprocity, I knelt at the foot of the bed and pulled her toward me. Her blood did not quicken quickly, but it seemed she deliberately prolonged it, for once the train had started up, she showed herself an expert engineer, and moved so beautifully against me it was a pleasure to be of use. At last, amid a thunder of vaginal puffs and belches, flinging me side to side between her swaying knees, she came like . . . what shall I say? . . . like a fast freight, the sounds not torn from but easing out of her, a long finish that rolled and rolled until it became a train I'd have ridden if I could have, and she finally shuddered and said, "Oh, God, that was really a good one."

———————

6th

The possible endings:
(1) he destroys the marriage, then drops her.
(2) he sets out to do this, but instead is "saved" by her, whether or not they are together in the end. What constitutes this salvation?
(3) she destroys him; once he has fallen in love, she leaves.

In the terminal stages, one of them might say, "It doesn't have to be like this."

———————

7th

A phone call first thing this morning; she will be over about one.

Now, at three, she has just called to explain that Joshua came home unexpectedly with tickets for the symphony, a gift from the chief of medicine.

I said, "He knows." She was silent, and I heard bells in the background. "Where are you?"

"I came to the store for milk."

"What did you do with the milk you had?"

"Poured it in the toilet."

I said, "He knows, doesn't he?"

She thought not.

At some point this whole thing will go out of control.

8th

And what is the punch line? Of course: Charlotte and Joshua don't have a particularly physical relationship at all; it's rather mechanical that way and has been for years. I am not the first or even the second of her digressions.

"Who?" I asked her, "the erotic artist?"

A rose bandanna appeared pulled up just below her eyes. "A couple of times."

"Great."

"Why do you say that?" But she laughed. "We were

both whores; he wanted me to buy his stuff, and I wanted him to sell us the best pieces.''

"Do you still see him?"

She shook her head. "Not since you. This is different. I wanted you right away.''

"Really?"

"At Lucy's. The minute I heard your voice. You knew it then, too, didn't you?"

"I knew it before." She laughed when I explained, was astonished, unaccountably aroused, asked if I would write about us.

"If you want."

In fact, she wants me to write about everything. She is endlessly intrigued by my work and likes to discuss the solitude and self-discipline it requires. "It's risky," she said the other day, "isn't it? You could do all this work and have it come to nothing."

"Financially nothing, sure."

This constituted a kind of heroism in her eyes, and when I mentioned the hero's fear of the morning, the shudder in his bowels each time he sits at the desk, or his stupefied fascination with the shadow of the penpoint, these only spoke of greater heroism still.

We lay silent a few moments and, like a complementary afterimage, found ourselves thinking about her husband. "Joshua enjoys medicine," Charlotte said, though neither of us had mentioned him.

"I'm sure it's interesting if you're into it."

"Why don't you like him?"

"I don't dislike him."

In Charlotte's analysis, she and I have remained desperate characters while Joshua has become stolid and dull, and she regularly hauls out the great ideologies of the sixties to defend us. "He always said he wouldn't get caught up working all the time. He used to be interested in things. Now he's like his father.''

She probably had a point, but in this dreary year that argument impressed me only with its exhaustion. Not that it hadn't been true once and wasn't still in some moisture-free, time-proof place, but here on earth, on the street outside the window beside my desk, history had left that one behind. The faithful still squatted on the Avenue and groveled in it to mock the rest of us, but the rest of us, we went on.

"All the same," I said, feeling protective of Joshua, "it's good to be devoted to something. I'm devoted to my work."

"But not that much."

She hadn't said it to hurt, she just didn't want to be left alone. I was three hours devoted, and though there were answers to that charge, I let them pass, suspecting that this dispassion accrued to my credit on a balance sheet somewhere and not wanting to seem as if I needed to make the point.

"I have to go," she said. "He's getting a few days off. We're going out of town until Monday."

"What does that mean?"

She shrugged without shrugging. How did she feel when she was with him? I didn't ask. I put on pants and a T-shirt to see her out. The street was cold on my bare feet.

"I like you," she said. It was the first time I'd felt any clumsiness in her, and I noticed that the limp was almost gone; she didn't wear the Ace bandage anymore.

We kissed goodbye like the lovers we have not quite technically become, and her unnecessary taillights wavered off down the street, brightening at every intersection. The underside of my tongue was sore. Perhaps it pleased me a little to think of her with Joshua.

———————

October 11

Lucy was on duty this weekend, Charlotte was with Joshua in Big Sur, Jimmy's job had just finished, the band was off, so here were the four of us together in the Dodge again, on the road Saturday morning by nine, loaded by quarter past, headed off for a day in the country. I drove, Donna manipulated the radio, Shaw rolled, but it was Jimmy Wax who made himself master of this ceremony, the gathering of the group.

Of us all, Jimmy is the least committed to the house (he could panic and leave in a minute), and the most dependent on it. Yet he is its imp and its soul, the only escape Donna, Shaw and I have from our impossible postures of pride and self-sufficiency. Even today, when I felt in Jimmy a suppression of more than the usual melancholy, he showed no loss of humor or enthusiasm, remaining on one level a giggling, ripped ten-year-old, regardless of what happened on others, squandering his final paycheck on vast quantities of sliced meat, cheese, mustard, bread, salads, pastries, six-packs of Heineken's, quarts of Wild Turkey, filling the Dodge with a sea of crumbs, rinds, spillage, ashes, empties and balls of greasy paper. He filled it also with laughter, asking questions only Jimmy Wax can ask: how big was Jerry's? did Charlotte come sweet or tart? what was Shaw's elusive gender: queer, castrato or just some transcendent form of chaste?

The bourbon horizontal at his mouth, Shaw made no haste to answer, but eventually lowered the bottle and handed it over the seat to Donna who, already quartz-eyed and holding between her lips a cigarette she'd forgotten about until the bottle mouth attempted to displace it, now found her other hand already committed to a stupendous wad of corned beef with bread handles, tried to laugh at her predicament, but on account of the cigarette could not until Shaw gallantly took it from between her lips, put it between his own and said to Jimmy, "Retired."

The driver laughed.

"And James," said Shaw, turning tables, "what's the music in Ms. Blumenthal's little chamber like?"

"Pianissimo," said Jimmy, the melancholy bubble smiling still, "andante."

Donna, afraid to open her mouth lest entire tubes of bologna and wheels of cheese issue forth in lieu of words, nevertheless said, "Man, she makes some weird noises."

"True," said Jimmy, "a quiet sort of gushing, wouldn't you say?"

"None of that beaklike friction of the foam," said the driver.

"Far from it," said Jimmy, "none of that cheap phosphorescent ecstasy for Lucille Blumenthal."

All laughed except Donna who did not think they should joke about this, was not even certain what they were joking about. Another goof on despair, she decided, a kind of humor she'd barely heard of before the day last spring she first met Shaw in the Med. She'd learned more about it since. It even touched her sometimes, making her laugh against her will at fears she'd never known she felt. And now, despite her misgivings, the jokes about Lucy, like the opening of a door Donna had not previously noticed, gave onto a room of sexual confession. They talked of those extraordinary nights and days one rarely mentions, of homosexual hours, of one's greatest orgasm (not one of which had occurred in conventional intercourse), of an orgy, a sibling, a threesome, of being molested as a child by an otherwise benign family friend. And with this Donna felt herself open, not sexually, but in her heart, for the flip side of despair was that she could say anything to these guys, and anything was all right. Watching TV with them at night, she would lean back against someone's knee, he would put a hand on her shoulder, and it was not about fucking; often she did not even know whose hand it was and didn't care. And with this indifference came a greater pleasure still, she forgot about herself.

The confessions had gone on, then gradually transformed into a discussion of love. Yet it began to seem to the driver (though the driver had changed several times by now) that the primary love for each other was the one presently constituted in the car. Though he didn't mention this, it appeared to be mutually understood, for as the afternoon darkened into dusk, their speech, fragmented and personal in the morning, slowly dissolved into a river, a confluence of four tributaries whose individual waters were at first distinguishable, then not, and at this point the subject became the group itself; someone said, "Why don't we go to Europe?" and immediately a house in Paris was imagined, filled with baguettes and cheese, domestic discourse was translated into French, and each career assumed its continental form. Not that they ever would have gone, but the projecting of a collective future seemed the easiest way of naming present, perhaps drunken, stuffed and stoned, yet undeniable feelings.

It was night. The conversation had given out, and the lit cabin of the car raced along dark country roads. On the long ride home, all except the driver fell asleep. He drove with the window open, the cold air keeping him awake, and he enjoyed the silence and the solitude and, especially, the responsibility for the safety of his sleeping friends.

———

12th

While Charlotte is away, I have started going up on the roof again with Donna's binoculars. Today I performed a simple formalizing experiment; instead of letting my gaze wander about aimlessly, I trained the glasses on one pair of Park & Shop doors and held them motionless for three-minute intervals: these twelve feet for these one-hundred eighty seconds, observer remains neutral, follows nothing.

Thus restricted, the field of vision produced startling symmetries and rhythms. A solid form would balance against its trembling reflection in a glass door; a man inside the supermarket, shoulders and head visible through a window, moved left across the top of the frame, while outside a German shepherd trotted right across the bottom. A car filled the binoculars, a woman in red climbed in, and when it drove away, it revealed a woman in green coming out of the store.

The experiment broke down, however, when a man about forty-five in a faded black suit, white socks and lank hair stepped out into the sunlight. If he'd kept moving, I would have let him go, but he stopped just outside the doors, pulled a cellophane package from his bag, tore it open, and quickly fingered a wad of lunch meat into his mouth. Appetite temporarily satisfied, he remembered he was going somewhere, and the binoculars followed. A green bottle appeared, the cap was twisted off, and he swallowed rapidly several times, continuing, then, soda in one fist, meat in the other, bringing the hands to his mouth in slow alternation. He headed south on Telegraph. Going where? His walk had more of time than distance in it, as if he did not want to be found standing still. He was one of those vacant men who appear in supermarkets with a small steak, a giant Coke and quart of Lucky Lager. Who can bear to look at the shopping carts of people who live alone? They buy steak and sugar, trying to be nice to themselves, or a barbecued chicken, three frozen blueberry tarts, chocolate milk and a *TV Guide*. Don't want to get maudlin, but . . . one artichoke, one ear of corn, one stick of butter, one whole crab, the *National Enquirer* and a box of ammo. Do these people recognize the affinity between us like frogs know tadpoles?

The man dropped the empty bottle and meat package into the bag and brought out a snak-pak of, I believe, Oreos, opened it like a grenade and walked along popping cookies into his mouth, one after another, with an experienced squeeze of the package. Finishing this, he bagged it, rolled the whole into a ball and dropped it in the gutter. He disappeared behind the sharp slant of the Pancake House roof as he headed back to his rented room.

And there are others. The woman who accosts people waiting in lines and screams at them the injustices she has suffered: her husband stole the kids, the state withholds her payments, she used to be beautiful. Now her face is like the torn edge of a soup can. She waits furiously on the corners of busy intersections, then storms across the street, turns and waits furiously to come back. Or the man I met one icy night on Shattuck Avenue, naked except for a wool coat with no buttons. Or the man without a face. Or the walking ear. And especially the subtler versions, the nervous eyes, the hideous clothing, the tiny vanities of dress and grooming that are agonies of failure.

The man in black appeared far away in a space between buildings and was gone again. These people stagger along the border of alcoholism and insanity and by dint of concentration hold a life together for ten or twenty years; then they slip quietly into disrepair. Do I know them as the caterpillar knows the butterfly? Does it show in my face already? It is not completely impossible for an intelligent young man to end up forty years old and living in a rented room, making instant coffee with a heating coil; he passes out drunk one night, smoking in bed, and the funeral home gives the family half off on cremation costs. The ashes are scattered at sea, the light gray flakes settling on the dark gray waves, and the fear welcomes him home.

The man in the black suit was gone, and I put down the binoculars because I was beginning to feel queasy from looking through them so long. They eliminate the peripheral vision that usually connects viewer to object, so that each floats in a separate space.

Now the streets were full of cars and the sidewalks with people. Everyone was going home. Are there people who do not deserve the evening? From whom it has been stolen in advance? The old man who owns the pink house at the end of the block tottered around his property picking up scraps of paper with a pointed stick. The sunset had exploded his walls into a gorgeous and violent rose, but either he did not notice, or he enjoyed this spectacular beauty nonchalantly.

———————

14th

Our meetings are already ritualized: a walk, talk, and a cup of coffee to renew the acquaintance, then we come to this room and inscribe on each other's body a sequence of gestures whose meaning is affection, but which brings Charlotte to hair-flying climax while I am left shrieking at my impotence.

She is patient, of course. She tells me to relax, it doesn't matter. We kiss. We fondle. We pretend not to care where this is leading. I pretend she does not disgust me. I pretend not to be terrified of my disgust. Slowly I am taken in by the pretense, and we try again, try to shove it in fast when it shows a little interest, but at the last moment it always ducks away and bashfully declines.

Then I scream at the fucking thing and keep screaming until even Charlotte is slightly freaked by what is going on. She says, "Darling, please, here," and takes it in her mouth where it joylessly empties itself an instant later. (A blow job is still a job, after all.) Then I hoist her legs over my shoulders and bend to the task. We listen to music for a while, she goes, and she is gone.

———————

15th

It went soft in her mouth today, and why not? I was almost pleased, for this puts things so much more succinctly than I ever could have. She asked, "What's the matter?"

A question without answers, yet I heard myself saying, "I think I'd like to see you under different circumstances." Surprised, for I hadn't intended to bring up anything like this, it was nevertheless easy to marshall arguments for the idea, to invest my voice with a sincerity that convinced. I said, "I want more time. It's cold this way. We're affectionate, but the structure is cold."

"I thought you were always too warm." She smiled, put a hand on my side. "I couldn't spend any more time without telling him."

"I don't want to talk about him."

"He's my husband."

"He's not mine." That was too harsh. "No, I understand, you have to think about that, but I couldn't say anything helpful."

And was this even what I wanted, more time, different time, nights together, or was it only a good blow job I was after? A blow job without equivocation and disgust?

"Do you think I should tell him?"

I said, "Doesn't he see other people, too?"

"No."

I looked at her.

"I mean he has, once. Once that I know of. Ah, look . . ." An indifferent gesture as if she didn't really care what her husband did.

That seemed to throw my calculations off. She looked so

92

sad and lovely. Her naked shoulders; hair dark and smooth, like a river at night. I could imagine Joshua seeing her like that and wondering what was wrong. Charlotte, having given me up (he found out somehow), is waiting for Joshua to come to bed. From across the room he sees this expression and thinks it means she wishes she were still with me. He doesn't know that it is worse than that, that to her the joy is gone from everything, and it all seems pointless, Joshua, Harold, all of them.

"I should go." She sat up and looked for her blouse.

I said, "Do you want to?"

"Want to what? Spend more time?" She nodded reluctantly. "Yes."

"Well, then . . ."

"That's easy for you to say." She was miserable. "I thought this was just going to be . . ."

I said, "So did I."

This went on for another thirty minutes, and when she left neither of us had climaxed, an ending I liked somehow.

———————

Friday

So without planning it, I've apparently committed myself to a course of action. Having offered to raise the stakes, I must play at the new level or drop out altogether if she passes. If I contain even the possibility of compromise, everything will be lost. Such rigor would be inconceivable without a plan. It is in the structure that I find my courage. So when she called tonight to say she could come over for an hour, I realized I could not permit it.

"Is he on duty?"

She said, "Yes."

"Then you could stay the night."

"He usually calls."

"Say you were in the shower."

A hesitation, "You could come here," this a crumb reluctantly offered.

I said, "How would you like that?" No answer. "Neither would I. I want you here."

"Why?"

Why? Why do people have to ask. "Because I'm getting involved in this, Charlotte, which means risk, which means vulnerability, while you've got a safe thing to fall back on."

"It's not so safe."

"Why not? Is something happening?"

"Nothing specific. No. I don't know what you want."

"Something ventured."

"Harold, I'm involved too. It's driving me crazy, is that enough involvement for you?"

Almost. "Then you should be able to arrange it."

"You mean tell him?"

"Tell, lie, whatever."

"I can't do that yet."

I said, "I know." Then a long pause contemplating this dead end, that strange telephone silence, the soft crackle of empty wires, murmurs of adjacent conversations. "Look," I said slowly, "I think the thing for us to do is wait until you've decided what you want."

"You mean not see each other?"

"For a while."

"I don't want to not see you."

"Neither do I. But I have to know what we're dealing with. For my own sake. Is that fair?"

She said nothing, but I assumed she was nodding, and then she said, "Yes."

After we'd hung up, I realized that I hadn't actually wanted her to come at all. I liked the situation just like this, which left me wondering what this was.

Sunday

Tonight after dinner Jimmy "took me aside" in that confidential way and said, "Listen, I think you ought to know, Charlotte's going to be spending some time with Joshua now."

That smacked of conspiracy. "Who told you to say this?"

He grimaced. Obviously he wasn't supposed to say.

I said, "Was it Charlotte?"

He nodded, "Yeah."

"Bullshit. You talked to her yourself? Tell me what she said."

"Okay, I didn't actually—"

"Then you don't know what you're talking about, do you, Jimmy? For a change."

That got him. "I know she isn't going to be seeing you anymore."

"Want to bet? Did she tell Joshua about me?"

"No, but—"

"Then she'll be back."

"Ah, come on man . . ." He didn't want to fight.

95

"She's trying to save her marriage. What's wrong with that?"

What futility. Why are people always trying to save things, time, nature, souls and string? Why not just let it go, let it all go. The river will bring more in a minute.

———————

Monday 10 P.M.

It is night and I can feel her wanting me. She would still like to make it work with him, but it seems already too late for that. She stands looking out their living room window, and she is not there. Her mind follows her eye down the slope of lights as far as the elbow of the Bay Bridge propped on Treasure Island, but the fingers are invisible, buried in Berkeley-Oakland. So she stops here, unsure of how to go on, and this snaps her back to the living room where Joshua is sitting on the couch, bare feet in the new rug, a joint between his lips, looking at slides of work an artist of theirs did last winter in Florence. She sits beside him, again, and he hands her the viewer. They are going to make love in a while. Being with Joshua is so easy that she is unhappy without noticing her unhappiness, and for the first time in her life she broods.

When they begin to touch, she watches his face and feels his way of knowing her. He knows how her clothing fastens and what she likes to do herself. He has always said she was selfish or self-indulgent, and now she believes that, in fact, she is. She knows where he will touch next and what he thinks arouses her. She puts her arms around him. She thinks about the grapefruit juice in the refrigerator, about Harold and about Joshua's body knotted up with medical school. She berates herself for thinking so much. She won't admit that she resents him, but she chastises herself for it, anyway.

He senses an impurity, pauses, and with her body she tells him to go on, making herself come so that he will, wanting his to be good, then doing what she can to help him relax and enjoy his exhaustion. Yet she is afraid that she cannot invest even these familiar gestures with enough feeling, that he can tell, and he can, but he does not know how to ask, to say, the words are difficult, and he is tired, they are tired. . . .

They sleep, but I do not. Sleep fixes these images in their thoughts, and I want to warn them against drifting off like this with the gas on. I could tell them stories from now until morning about couples who asphyxiated waiting for the air to clear. I dislike this carelessness with their marriage. Have they had such an easy time of it that they can afford to squander a good thing? What do they think comes next? Maybe someone should wake them up to what is going on here.

But "Oh," they would say if I did, "You don't know how sick of this I am, the same shit over and over, and frankly I haven't the strength for it, anymore. I thought relationships were supposed to make things easier, but this is just dragging us down. I'm not sure we both wouldn't be better off living separately for a while and seeing if . . ."

Do you think so? All right, I won't bother you with my advice. Sleep. I have my patience to keep me company, and patience may soon emerge from her cocoon as one of you, and then the other will be, as he says, better off.

97

21st

Still no word from her, and now I wonder if I haven't over-estimated the effects of the childhood farm. Maybe a suburb was closer than I thought, enclosed her in its school district (that's what happened to Donna) and threw my calculations off. Maybe there weren't enough of those long afternoons reading Emily Bronte beneath a willow. (Are there even willows in the Santa Cruz Mountains?)

No willows, no mountains, just those vast tracts of ranch houses Californians cram onto their rolling countryside, and Charlotte walking home from school in a tartan skirt, notebooks held against her chest like an infant.

At the Friday-night canteen the popular girls stand in a group, their eyes scanning the gym as they whisper together. Charlotte is among them because she is pretty and sweet and the girls have heard the boys talking about her. She doesn't say much, but she listens. She learns, to her amazement, that boys (like girls) are commodities, their value determined by the status each confers on the girl he agrees to like. Charlotte thinks this is ridiculous. Alan Sampson, for instance, seems to her a bully with a weak chin. She can't understand why the other girls think he's a dream. She's confused, even angry (does Charlotte get angry?) and imagines telling her mother about it when she gets home. The thought comforts her, and she feels less alone. But a moment later Harriet Markle sees Bobby Buchannan (a conceited moron in Charlotte's book) strut by and says into Charlotte's ear, "God, he's cute, huh?"

Charlotte is so flattered to be the recipient of this intimacy from the magnificent Harriet (whom she thinks really is beautiful and cool) that she happily nods, mumbles, "unh huh," and hopes that doesn't count as a lie.

So that night she doesn't tell her mother anything, and today she doesn't call me. Society is a language we all learn.

There is a moment in the career of every woman (of a particular class and type) when she is obliged to choose between passion and security. And just as the mongoose always gets the cobra, these women always make the same choice. Yet it is one of those exquisitely contrived dramas in which an outcome that was prefigured in the creation appears uncertain up to the last moment, in this way yielding a maximum in suspense without exposing them to any actual risk.

And do they make the wrong choice? I wouldn't say that. If it is the one they make, it must be right. I applaud its rightness and her prudence. It is, as she said, the only way.

I could write to her, but I won't. Let silence be my speech.

Charlotte   Dear Charlotte,

I hear from Jimmy that   Jimmy has conveyed   Jimmy has delivered your message, and I suppose that beyond any personal   Jimmy has delivered your message and beyond any personal disappointment or pain, I think you're doing the right thing.

I think it's the right thing. There's a moment in the life of every woman when she has to choose between passion and security   between security and passion,   between what has substance and history and what is only a potential.

The trouble is it was so delicious as far as it went it's hard to give up going further. I can still smell your hair on the pillow, your cunt on the sheets. Maybe I even still hear echoes of . . .

Charlotte, listen, there is a moment in the life of

everyone when he has to choose between passion and security. Think of being 50 and having chosen security. Think of the dead lives. Charlotte, there is a way with terror on either side, but at the end . . . I don't know the end. I only know   that this is the way.

Dear Charlotte

———————

22nd

Maurice Ronet sits still, his eyes poised on an aperitif someone has left unfinished on the table next to his. He glances around the cafe to see if anybody is watching.

The film was being projected onto a screen that hung in front of a huge picture window in the public events lounge of Merritt College, high in the Oakland hills. No one had closed the curtain between them, so all around the black and white rectangle, the city of Oakland spread out in a lavender panorama, the hills of Marin now purple humps against a Pyribenzamine sky, cars pouring off the east end of the Bay Bridge.

Ronet reaches for the abandoned drink and swallows it. The movement is simple, yet a moment later he shudders and is dead. An intermittent drizzle of Satie notes falls throughout the scene, muting the emotion. The shudder passes, Ronet looks around, but he is dead. In a sense, the rest of the film does not matter. You see that man over there, someone across the cafe says of Ronet, the one with the eyes, he used to be beautiful.

Beneath the screen a river of lights moved along the MacArthur Freeway; pieces broke away from the mass and flickered off down local roads. The people the world was made of were going home.

Maurice Ronet meets a powerful businessman at a dinner party. They insult each other. The hostess, a former lover, tells Ronet, G____, you know, he is a force of nature. Oh, well, says Ronet, I am not a force of nature.

Each car found its house and stopped. Inside dinner was served.

Maurice Ronet finishes reading *The Great Gatsby*, takes a pistol from his suitcase and presses the nose of the barrel to his chest. Hairs squirm under the metal. Cut away to the opposite wall: some books on a shelf, a piece of a window, branches. A pistol shot. Satie sprinkles the screen. End titles. Maurice Ronet is congratulated on a fine performance.

The house lights came back on, and the purple city became a black reflection of the public events lounge. I went out to the parking lot, got in the Dodge and drove back to Berkeley.

Behind the curtains of the Portuguese house the woman had finished the dishes. The kid was doing his homework. The man wanted to get his hands on his wife, so he said, "Listen, kid, isn't it time for bed?" The kid looked up at his mother. She smiled sadly. The man saw this and exploded with rage. Okay, things were not benign even in the chocolate Portuguese house; the man had alcohol in his blood, terror in his bowels, loathing in his cock. But to the question of the morning he could always say: I must. Necessity gave him meaning, while I was beyond necessity. As Shaw had explained recently, I had no relation whatsoever to the means of production. Who would starve if I never wrote another word? Not even I. I was superfluous even to myself. And already I was twenty-six.

Friday

She should have gotten the letter yesterday, today at the latest. It is already past five o'clock. Joshua gets home about six, so if she is going to call, it has to be within the hour. If not, Monday is the soonest, and I won't wait that long. At six I will go for a walk and be done with this. It is six. It is quarter past. It is ten to seven. I pronounce it dead.

I walked. The night was thick, impenetrable. As in a maze, each street turned back on itself, and the more anxiously I sought new routes and unknown directions, the quicker these inverted toward home: crescents, loops, streets that turned to rubble and stopped, streets that led to streets that opened onto an intersection four blocks from the house when I'd thought I must be miles away. My palm came wet off my hair; water had soaked through my shoes. At home I went to change and found Charlotte lying where I am lying now, reading in this notebook where I am writing.

I put out the light, undressed and fucked her as easily as if my dick were a riderless horse that just followed its nose home. A breeze blew through the window and up my inverted ass, cooling and drying those angry hairs. I have awakened later and am writing by light from a street lamp. I still have no idea how she's arranged this.

———————

Sunday

Lucy was driving up to Mendocino to visit friends, and since Joshua had weekend duty, Charlotte said she would go along. It is the kind of thing they do every so often. Lucy dropped her here on the way out Friday and picked her up coming home today. Terrifying how easy it is.

For most of the weekend we hardly spoke, save a continuous trickle of sounds more like touches than words, and that rather sustained the silence than interrupted it. Likewise, I don't remember anything we did so much as the effortless way it all occurred, one movement transforming smoothly into the next without any holes in the fabric of events. Often I had the sense that Charlotte was leading me through a complex ritual in which every gesture was prescribed, every moment accounted for. I never turned and reached for something without knowing exactly how fast to move my hand or with which fingers I should grip it; each time I spoke, the perfect words were waiting, and they invariably found the tone and inflection that suited them best. The ritual was so subtle it seemed almost spontaneous, yet it took care of every contingency and spared us the anxiety of thinking about what to do next.

Saturday afternoon we walked up into the hills, and on the way Charlotte would point to this leaf or that sound in the brush and call it gingko or ground squirrel, would call the odor eucalyptus; the yellow, Scotch broom; the heat, Indian summer—words whose sounds interested me far more than the objects they named. I silently repeated, ''sparrow hawk,'' and without taking my eyes from the ground, pictured a large, black falcon scouring the clouds for its meals. "Can they really catch sparrows?"

Charlotte laughed, pointed, "Look," and I saw a small, brown *t* spiralling above the gulley where we stood. It was somewhat like a sparrow itself (I tried to believe) though more methodical, halting a moment in midflight, going, halting, then seeming to copy in the air the movement of something on the ground until it precipitously dropped, to the earth, then rose again, a fragment of the ground rising with it, or so Charlotte said, "Look," indicating an object squirming in the hawk's talons, Charlotte's face luminous with fear and delight.

"What is it?"

"A chipmunk, a mouse," she said.

Above the gulley we reached a level stretch of woods and fields and lay together in the high grass. Unseen things crawled all around us; I was frightened, and Charlotte said not to be, it was nothing; sometimes there were snakes, but not this late in the year. "Don't be afraid. Listen." There were two sounds, there were twenty, there were two hundred. She said, "Look." There was a long slope faded to a monotonous brown where, a moment later, clumps of yellow flowers sprang up everywhere Charlotte pointed, the whole expanse then clouded with a purple haze she called lupine. Even shit (we were up and walking again) marked the passing of deer and coyote, the park suddenly filled with animals I'd never dreamt inhabited it. The only nature I had ever looked at voluntarily were the endless varieties of sky and light that divided the year; occasionally a mountain or tree might force itself on my consciousness, but I have never noticed the minutiae. Now Charlotte would stoop and lift something, and against her fingers would appear a green net so subtle that it vanished when my head moved, changing the angle of sunlight. Or she would run a pine needle along the enameled orange of a beetle wing, the color breaking sharply redward toward the tip, as though an almost erotic struggle were occurring at the level of pigment.

And while Charlotte's eyes continued to inspect this exquisite detail, I, hardly having seen the thing itself, was already greedily scanning the ground for more, taking a rapid census of all plant and animal life in the vicinity, wishing to possess not only the names of everything I could lay eyes on, but also the numerous biological relationships, the arrangements of space, weight and color (which Charlotte made vivid, like Duchamp, simply by holding up a frame before what was already there) and, especially, the varieties of time, the time of the deer, the petal, the wasp and the rock, all laminated in a single instant. For a few seconds I thought I had hold of all this, but there was too much; the profusion of forms collapsed into Abundance, the numberless times into Time, and my mind, too restless for One and too weak for Every, settled for that blandest of compromises, All.

I looked up and found myself alone in a small clearing. I said, "Charlotte?" There was no answer. Then among some foliage twenty yards away appeared a patch of roan, and above it, two blue eyes locked to mine. For a moment I thought it was a fox or a deer, its shape concealed by protective coloring. Then I saw that it was Charlotte. I had wandered away from her without realizing it, and looking back, she became, for an instant, no longer the woman I had known this morning, but part of the forest. Her face was alert, yet nearly blank, and reduced to that one expression from which all others were derived: she was erotic, erotic as she stood, as the dark hair blew in a cup around her perfect ear, as she looked back across the clearing not at me, Harold Raab, but at this briefly unknown other, bestowing on him all the eroticism of her gaze.

I want to say that I loved her there, but it was not that simple. There I, not Harold, loved her, not Charlotte. There the ritual reached its conclusion and the erotic spread through everything like the physicists' old ether.

That should have been enough, but I realized that the love on Charlotte's face (and, presumably, on mine) was for something so basic it might have belonged to anyone, just as the salt in one person's blood assumes the same crystal structure it has in anyone else's. And I did not want to be loved for what was universal in me, but for what was particular, nor for what was lovable, but what was loathesome. And what is loathesome in a lover always seems to be those particulars that make for otherness. It was only at that distance, then, sixty feet or so, that a universal love was possible. Up close the breath smelled.

With that the branches, the clearing, the blue air reappeared between us, and the love was gone. I put an arm around her waist, and Charlotte smiled, tucking in the corners of her mouth as though to suppress a larger smile still. She tugged at my sleeve, I squeezed her biceps, and we walked back down the hill toward home.

That night I thought I smelled Joshua on her, the whiff of an odor that wasn't hers, and on her body I found the marks other men had made. There were lovers in her hands, in her mouth and in the way she moved. Her body was a history of lovers; I hadn't realized she'd had so many. She had learned to do this when she was twenty, had found she liked that there, here she'd been hurt and was still wary. Now I was inscribing my mark, and she, no doubt, was leaving hers on me, marks that would always be there like initials cut in a tree, and that, years from now, we might still patiently discern beneath all the intervening signatures.

How effortless a fuck can be. Saturday night we reached a place where coming came of its own, unpursued. Sunday that was already lost, and we grasped at each other furiously until the climax was torn from unwilling and bruised flesh. It's true that sex is never enough; even when the last fuck of life has shot through us, there will be something left behind it didn't get.

"What time is it?" she said.

"Almost noon."

"Lucy'll be here soon."

A church bell struck eleven times; daylight savings had ended giving us an extra hour. I held her waist, pressed her stomach against mine, we tried to touch everywhere at once, fingers in every hole.

"You go so deep," she said.

"I want to go all the way."

"Yes, go all the way." But that was impossible; the cunt wasn't deep enough, I wasn't long enough, it was only inches and minutes. I was outside her and always would be, and it was not enough to be outside, I wanted to get in there.

———————

27th

Is fucking enough? "Enough for what?" asks Shaw, though he knows what I mean. Jimmy withdraws into his room these days, and Donna is rarely home, but Shaw encourages that necessary perversion, speech, without which the other pleasures fade.

"Could you make a religion out of it? Or a career?"

"People have."

"Flaubert gave everything to art, and that seems at least as stupid."

"Having a good time, huh."

I arrive at my desk, settle into the chair and think of Charlotte. A dreamy hour later, the top buttons of my shirt are open, and I find myself fingering the nipple of my left breast. The day is overcast. I hear a plane I cannot see, and it occurs to me that a few thousand feet up the weather vanishes, and everything is unequivocally blue.

I drop my pants and hold the wastebasket between my knees. I am saying "blonde" or "the blonde" though Charlotte is not blonde, nor am I picturing any woman with blonde hair. There is a hollow pattering as I ejaculate onto the papers in the wastebasket. An errant spasm streaks my jeans, and I rub it into the fabric with three fingers which I am now idly sniffing while I write this with the other hand. I have done nothing for days. When I think about my life it seems I should panic because I am certainly going to be an utter failure, but lately it is difficult to care. Fucking seems the only consideration, and once I am inside her this afternoon, all the rest will recede to its appropriate insignificance. Fucking is the blue; the rest is just weather.

30th

Now we are together nearly every day except weekends, which she says are torture, and gradually she arrives earlier and leaves later until it seems she goes home only to eat, sleep and sign in. How could Joshua not know? One morning she appeared at ten-thirty with a picnic lunch in a wicker basket, and I thought, my God, this woman is going to eat me, she will eat my entire life, doesn't she have anything else to do with herself? She was disappointed when I said I had to work until noon. Had to? She didn't think I had to, and couldn't today be an exception? It could not. Angry and hurt, this was Joshua all over again, she said she'd wait downstairs. I stared at the page for fifteen minutes, weighing the discipline of work against the discipline of flexibility, found the latter more difficult and, in this instance, truer to an ethic that, if I could not practice in my life, I would not be able to depict in my work—so that ultimately both principles led one way, and I turned off the lamp.

But Charlotte and I are not much preoccupied with theoretical issues. Usually we are in bed ten minutes after she drives up and don't get out until she leaves, less occasional forays after food, and even these are infrequent since our bodies provide nourishment as well as activity. I am thinking of buying a chamber pot so we can piss and shit right here. I want to watch the turds open her anus and see the urine poise like rain on the fine branches of her nest. I want to say things the page cannot tolerate.

We explore our bodies like children and have rapidly acquired fluency in each other's corporal dialects. I study her labia as if character could be divined from the folds; those wrinkled, purply lips seem the oldest thing on her, centuries older than the rest, as if they have been passed down from woman to woman since the origin of the gender, old cunts in new bodies. I have pushed them open to watch her lubricate, and it pulsed out in such pungent, milky waves that I told her it was her odor I loved first. She laughed and said she never smelled so strong until she met me.

We have developed not only the usual repertoire of positions, but numberless fantasies for each one. We have virginal fucks; betrayal fucks; deadly, insect fucks; the slow, swooning fucks of mythical birds, fucks that flush the brain; Marxist fucks; baseball fucks; winter fucks; Tuesday fucks; Proustian fucks; fucks standing between drying sheets in the cold March sunshine; love fucks; banana fucks; farewell fucks; Mathilde de la Môle fucking El Greco fucks; sweet summer corn fucks; and this is only the beginning, or the middle, and fucking but a single phase of the moon. There are other orifices and ideas, convex and concave parts, skin, nail, tendon, tooth. There is blood, there is tongue, there is sphincter, there is leather, there are apples and whips. (No whips yet.) She gives me her mouth, her ass, the hollow behind her knee. I particularly wanted to come in her hair, thinking it would be beautiful to see white semen shoot through that dark mass, but my climax was so unbearable I could not look. I came rock, and when it finally stopped, sperm was running down into her eyes, and she said, "Darling, you come so sad."

I don't think it is sad exactly, but there is a strange, mute irony to sex, something it always holds back. Our inventive delights all lead to one end, and as we come, as we start to, in the moment that sharpest wave breaks, I am thinking: is this it? is it God? what is this? do I care? I don't care. What's the difference? So what. . . .

No, that's not quite it. I want to know what that sensation is and why it's like that; I want to penetrate the experience, to fuck coming, as it were, but the moment I try to understand, it is as if my effort punctured the thing, it deflated, and I am left wondering why I have made so much of so little.

When I woke this afternoon, she was already dressed, standing over the desk, writing a note. I closed my eyes and listened to her go: feet on the stairs, the front door, the gate, sidewalk, car door, ignition, acceleration, shift and the cl-click, cl-click of the turn signal before she disappeared into the general roar of traffic.

The note said: "I want you to do everything to me." Even kill you?

In the fold were a dozen shining pubic Cs, standing, I presumed, for "Charlotte" or "cunt" or both or some for one and some for the other. Of course, I could not really hear the turn signal. I sat naked at the desk, fingering my loose dick, and heard the Simca whine up the block and bounce over the lip of its driveway. Then I heard its door, the garage door, screen door, front door of the Portuguese house, and, finally, the clatter of metal runners as the curtain closed over the bedroom window. Maybe they were going to fuck before dinner. Of course, I couldn't really hear the curtain, but when I looked up, it was closed. Everything. Portuguese woman fucks. Charlotte and the Portuguese woman together. Let me count the ways.

November 1

My roommates don't like her. They don't say so, won't even intimate it, but there is an awkwardness when Charlotte arrives and silence after she has gone. Maybe they disapprove of what I'm doing or resent the attention I give her. Donna probably thinks Charlotte is too straight and typically feminine, "cowy," she would say, and Jimmy, whose vocabulary is larger, thinks "cloying" or "insipid," while Shaw, of course, doesn't care who I fuck.

None of this affects the routine. We still eat together, go to the movies, hang out. Yet even with Shaw I've felt a change lately, something between us or something not.

Late last night I asked if he wanted to go out for coffee. He said, "Fine," but once in our usual booth in the Pancake House told me, "I can't stay too long. I've got to get up tomorrow."

I said, "What for?"

"I have a class at ten."

"Class?" I felt a panic. "A class of what?"

"For my job. Didn't I tell you about this?"

I shook my head, amazed.

"It's not a job exactly. I'm just running a couple of poli-sci sections for a friend. One of his TAs got hepatitis, and there was no one else qualified in the department. . . ." He shrugged. "Anyway, we need the money."

"So what does that mean? You're going back to finish your dissertation or something?"

"I doubt it. We'll see how this goes."

"I'm amazed you didn't tell me."

"I thought I had." He smiled. "Anyway, you've been busy."

"Not all the time."

Shaw shrugged.

"You don't mind, do you?"

He looked at me in astonishment. Mind? Shaw? On what possible grounds?

I said, "I want to ask you something a little awkward."

"Sure."

"What do you think of her?"

"Charlotte?" He thought a minute. "I don't really know her. She seems like a nice girl. She has a beautiful ass."

"Thanks."

"I wasn't complimenting you."

"And you don't have any moral problems about Joshua or anything? . . ."

Shaw snorted with amusement.

I said, "Jimmy does."

Shaw made the condescending gesture he often uses in reference to Jimmy. "Jimmy still thinks that if he's a good boy and upholds the moral order, the world will bestow its rewards on him, and his Mom'll be impressed."

I laughed, and we kept talking, but it wasn't the same. Everything Shaw thought and didn't say accumulated between us. He doesn't understand that with Charlotte all the criteria are new. And if I'd tried to explain, he still wouldn't have gotten it, and I'd only have demeaned myself by trying.

2nd

A letter from my father today. Actually just a note, "Take a look at this:" attached to a newspaper clipping about two semifamous former Weathermen who've "dropped back in" and are opening a chain of cafeteria-style French restaurants in the Washington, D.C., area. Get the picture? Yes, we see.

And because I'm a mature guy and feeling a bit less shitty these days, I decided not to take this as an insult or provocation. Instead I wrote back a nice, chatty letter in which I pretended that these assholes with their restaurants didn't make me want to weep blood. In short, I tried to pass myself off as just the sort of thoughtful, temperate twerp my father wishes I were. Which self-restraint left me so awash in humiliation and rage that I tore my reply to shreds and pasted the clipping to our refrigerator door just below Jimmy's mother's famous letter.

November 3

She thinks Joshua is showing the effects, though he still doesn't know what's affecting him. (See how she is learning from me.) He withdraws from her instinctively, and while this tortures her, she cannot make herself reach out to him in the old way; she is actually relieved to be left alone. What should she do?

I said, "Tell him what's happening."

"Maybe we should stop seeing each other."

I looked at her.

"What then?"

"What do you want?"

She put her arms around me.

I said, "What else?"

"I don't know."

"Then maybe we should stop."

"I can't. I want to, but I can't."

Great. "Why not?"

"Don't you know?"

I shook my head, but suddenly I didn't want to hear this.

"You care about everything so much. You think you plan it all in that book of yours, but it's really just something inside driving you. Don't you know how exciting that is?"

"Then what's the problem?"

"I can't stand what it's doing to Joshua."

I said, "Tell him. The worst part's not knowing."

She shook her head. "I have to make up my mind."

But she won't. She'll balance passion against responsibility, find them equal and continue as before. Raising the question is her act of atonement. Okay, yes, I like watching her squirm a little. She's seeing a different side of things, and, as I promised Lucy, this is good for her.

Thursday

Late yesterday afternoon, when she had only forty-five minutes before picking up Joshua, we met briefly on the couch in Lucy's apartment. And as I was about to come, I paused a moment, like Shaw with his firebomb, not simply to wait for her, but to observe this wave rising in me.

Climax changes with proximity. That morning when we'd arranged the meeting, it had seemed only a distant pleasure, one among many. But the urgency grew during the day (fed with phone calls), until by the time Charlotte let me into the apartment we were naked almost before the door had closed, and I was inside her at once. Yet at that point the momentum began strangely to reverse, and I found myself trying to postpone what until then I had so desperately wanted. At first this seemed a matter of consideration or performance, but as climax became imminent, then inescapable, as the wave swelled and rose, I began to see a monster in it. It wasn't pleasure at all coming at me, but a wave of pelvic granite that would tear me open and shatter me.

Meanwhile, a very different sort of orgasm was leaking its slow way through Charlotte, and she, so attentive to me at the beginning, now floated off too busy to pay attention. Unless, as she claimed later, her apparent indifference was actually its opposite, that being so fully possessed by me, suffused with me, nothing she thought or did was "about" anything else. When she said, "You fill me up, Harold, not just there," my entire body seemed to have become a liquid ejaculated into her and now slowly dispersing through her tissue.

Yet however possessed or suffused, Charlotte could not at the time have appreciated my difficulties with this approaching wave. Specifically, I had no idea where to go or how to get out of its way. But it was much too late for that; it was turning over on itself, and here I was coming razor blades and fire hydrants, unheard of things that wouldn't fit but forced themselves anyway until, unable to endure any more of this spastic madness, I looked up over the arm of the couch at the trees in Lucy's park.

Every needle was burned against the melon sky as if by a laser, and the huge, black cones seemed not trees but masses of feeling (peace, pain, an intolerable clarity) with which I had filled them to spare myself the full force of the orgasm, passing that sensation on to them, letting the lesser waves roll through me, the trees and I beating afterward to a single pulse.

And as the sensation faded, my sense of cowardice grew (the wave no longer seemed a monster at all) until Charlotte's hoarse voice said, "Darling, it's late, I have to go, but oh, my God. . . ." Which was, in effect, the backwash of the wave, catching me unaware, knocking me flat. It hadn't frightened Charlotte; she'd have gone with God if he'd called.

Then out of the dark her face rose, not even a face, really, just two liquid glimmers in the eyes, another on the surface of her teeth. I pressed against her thinking: one more inch and I will burst through into her, knowing I would not, that it was just the straining I was after.

———————

November 7

A moment ago I answered the phone, and almost without a hello she asked if I knew of any small apartments for rent in Berkeley. Any rentals to share? I went blank under the enormity of the question. She affected a businesslike manner and apologized for interrupting my work. I played along, said goodbye and came back to the desk. But what does this mean?

"It means," she said, "that I've been thinking about living on my own for a while."

I said, "Good idea."

"Do you think so?"

"What's wrong?"

"Nothing."

Strangely we were still dressed and sitting on the edge of the bed. I said, "Charlotte . . ." we kissed, but then she seemed to move away. So that was it: no husband, no lover; give me up to pay for the crime; return the goods and cop a plea.

She said, "I need some space for myself."

117

I'd had it with that space shit. "What space, this?" indicating the distance now between us on the bed.

"I don't know."

I said, "Come here."

She came, but she also held back. "What's happening to me is hard."

I said, "Tell me."

"I wouldn't know what to say. It isn't you, Harold, it's just me."

It wasn't me? "Try."

She tried hard. She rose up out of herself, I said, come here, and she came, then I whispered . . . but I cannot say what I whispered, though it's obvious, isn't it? I said things I shouldn't have, too much, whatever came to mind, until, finally, she was really throwing herself into it, holding hard and loving me, she said, loving her darling, while I was going to make her come sixty times or until she was dead, whichever came first. Back in high school they had said, eat her once and she's yours forever, belief in the principle enduring despite inflation and countless refutations.

In the end, however, I don't think it was sixty times, maybe three or two or just one good one with rolling hills to either side. But it was enough to take her face apart and put it back together soft. Then we lay silent a while. She pulled the covers up over her shoulder. I freed my leg. The problem was still there, it just didn't hurt anymore. Codeine.

She said, "I should live alone for a while, shouldn't I?"

I said, "Yes." I looked at her arm lying across my chest and wondered what it meant there. Had she put it there consciously? Did she accept responsibility for every second that it remained? How many of those seconds were lies? How many inertia? Her hand turned so that the fingertips touched the skin over my ribs, and briefly this reassured me, but when some time had passed without further movement, I became suspicious again.

Then she took the arm away, got up and stepped into her panties. She pulled a shift over her head, knotted the belt, laced her sandals. She said, "What about tomorrow?"

I said, "Call me."

———————

9th

Sometimes, as I poise above her, it occurs to me that at this moment (a Monday afternoon at two-thirty) Joshua is at the hospital being a doctor while I am here playing in bed.

He is examining a gynecology patient, say, touching her gently and asking questions and giving his diagnosis to the chief gynecology resident, John Kerner, as well as to the other medical students making rounds. For the moment Joshua is so utterly absorbed in the patient that he forgets his preoccupation with the problem of Charlotte.

He completes the diagnosis, infers from Kerner's mild emendations that he has done very well and is startled to realize that he did not really need Kerner to confirm that. He understood the patient, knew the medicine, put it together. It is simple, yet this sudden vision of his own competence seems unbearably bright. He disclaims it to himself, silently pronounces several magical modest phrases to stave off the jinx of hubris, and, nevertheless, rations himself a tiny morsel of pride.

He is happy. As the group continues down the corridor, sunlight pouring through windows at the far end, Joshua's body feels like it used to in his rugby days, every cell alive and moving. He smiles at two classmates passing in the hall.

One is Lucy. The other is a girl from Boston he has always liked and who, he now sees, likes him, too. Her smile follows him a bit more than is perfunctory. Now, finally, his thoughts return to Charlotte, but instead of the familiar dread, he feels only a lighthearted indifference whistling through him. Whatever is coming there, let it come.

Tuesday

Lucy's conscience is bothering her. Finding her couch damp with the residue of our exotic vespers the other evening, she began to regret not simply the apartment key she had given Charlotte that morning, but whatever small part she has played in this from the start.

So she called me up, and we had lunch today in a restaurant called the Knuckle, dark-paneled, German, filled at noon with white medical coats and beer. I said, "What do you want from me?"

"Stop seeing her."

I said, "This is about you and Jimmy, right?"

A short movement of her hand: it had nothing to do with that. "Joshua's dying," she said.

"What's he got, cancer?"

"Don't be an asshole."

Dying; she sounded like Joshua himself. Why does everything people say and do seem overacted? "Dying" was a lie that exposed itself like a flasher.

"Look," she said, "it was funny for a while, but it's serious now. This is a terribly destructive thing you're doing."

Now that one hurt. Not that it was any less bullshit than the rest, but it sounded enough like my mother to summon a vision of myself as one of those bulbous and warted trolls who makes miserable the life of the fairy princess.

I said, "You miss the point. I'm into this."

Ah, what a stalemate Lucy and I are. By countless means and from countless angles she tried to persuade me that she knew I was not, and I tried to discover why she cared. Neither of us made headway. Eventually she said, "Think about it, Harold. I have to get back."

On the way out we ran into Joshua Cobin who looked bad indeed, but greeted us cheerfully. "He can't even figure out why he's so miserable," she said when we were outside. In the drizzly daylight Lucy didn't look too good herself; deep purple pouches had sunk below her eyes, and the veins stood out like ant tunnels on her wrists. I realized that I missed seeing her.

I said, "Come on, Lucy, who are you really looking out for with this business?"

She thought a minute, then as if surprised by her own answer, said, "You."

11th

First-rate today, maybe even a little too good, considering. We stamped out another high-quality fuck and could go on like this forever, but what is the point? What are the possible points?

A bad one. Like Freud, my grandmother has cancer of the jaw. A year ago they thought they got it all, but tonight my father called to tell me that a lump has now appeared at the base of her tongue and that she had to be admitted to a hospital in Miami. The doctors are afraid the liver may be involved. They are flying her back to Philadelphia tomorrow.

I said, "How long do they give her?"

"Growth rates vary," said Manny, "they won't predict."

"Approximately."

"I'd say six months if we're lucky."

"What about your father?"

"He's pretty good."

"Does he know?"

"He knows she's in the hospital. I think he probably suspects."

I said, "Manny, does she know?"

"I'm sure she does."

"Has anybody told her?"

"We're waiting for a consulting opinion on the frozen slide."

"And then what?"

Finally he was angry. "And then I'll talk it over with my sister and anybody else in the family who cares enough to be here."

I said, "Do you want me to come east?"

"I'd like you to see her before she dies."

"What about Christmas?"

"Christmas is all right," he said. "Sooner might be better."

"I'll see what I can do."

"Fine."

"What's the matter?"

"The matter?"

"You seem upset."

"What do you think? My mother's dying. I'm upset."

"Yeah, all right."

"What?"

"Nothing. I'll call you in a couple days."

"Goodnight."

And then? Then Emmanuel Raab hangs up and exhales through rubber lips. My mother asks him, What's the matter? He looks at her, washboard brow and weary eyes, shakes his head. What did he say? He said he'll see. Frances makes a face which, while not happy, is nevertheless unsurprised, and she returns to her reading. But Manny cannot put the conversation aside. His son, he now realizes, made no remark of sadness or commiseration, expressed no regret about his grandmother, and this coldness burns Manny's heart with a delicious pain, a pain in which he finally locates his own elusive grief. He tries to think of his mother, but it is his son who preoccupies him. He thinks, if only the boy would. . . .

No, I can't do Manny. I can't be fair.

12th

She was supposed to be here at one-thirty, and now has just called at two to say she can't make it.

"Can't?"

"I don't want to."

"You know we haven't seen a whole lot of each other lately."

She said, "I miss you."

"Well, what do you think is going on?"

A silence in which, "I'm depressed," simply shortened the time required to say she had no answer.

"About Joshua?"

"Sort of. . . . No, about me. I don't like myself right now."

"Do you want me to come over there?"

No, she wanted to think. Well, let her think, but this sad-eyed lady skit is getting to be a bummer. Much too sensitive for a rotting soul like mine. Lady, please, says Lee, I haven't got the time.

Dear Manny,

I didn't mention it on the phone the other night, but I'm sorry about your   but I was sorry to hear about your mother's, my grandmother's, to hear that Grandma Flora is . . .

Dear Manny,

I know how you must feel about your mother, and I'm sorry. She is dying. The death of one's mother . . . Who am I kidding?

Dear Manny,

Am not sure; what are my grief obligations vis-à-vis your mother and her imminent demise? Am I supposed to feel sorry for her (i.e., that she is sick, in pain, dying) or for myself (that I am losing a loved one) and/or for others (e.g., the human beings in the family who still feel the proper emotions)? Or something else? Please advise by return mail, and I will do my best to . . .

Dear Manny,   Dear Dad, Dear Father, Pop, Papa   Dear Daddy, Dada   Goo goo   Gugu Wawawawawawawa. . . .

15th

Two days without a word, then she called and wanted to come over. I said no. No? If I'd told her I was busy, she might have known it was a lie, but it would have been easier to take.

"What are you doing?"

I said, "Come on, Charlotte, I'm tired of this."

She said, "I feel good."

"Today? How come?"

"I don't know. I want to see you. Have you been outside yet? It's beautiful."

I looked out the window.

"I'll be there in forty minutes."

I said, "I can't today. I'm working, then I'm going out to dinner."

She was silent.

I said, "Maybe Wednesday."

"Harold. . . ."

"Not right now."

She hung up. It rang again, and she said, "I'm sorry."

I didn't know what to say. She begged to be tortured. "I can't talk to you right now. Give me a day or two."

A pause. "All right." She waited. "I love you."

It was all a lie. My side of it. Hers, too, probably.

———

16th

Actually there was one truth: I did have a date for dinner. Pamela Marcus had called the day before, and since I hadn't been up to see them in several months, I accepted. And, as usual after an evening with the Marcuses, I feel ascetic today.

Noah is seventeen months old and already approximates Pamela's "fuck, man" for his all-purpose exclamation. Mickey just had a prison article in *Rolling Stone* and is now on assignment for the *Voice*. All my friends are moving from the flatlands up to the hills, and eventually they topple over the ridge into Los Angeles or New York. The Marcuses lean toward the latter because more journalism is done there and now that Pamela's paintings have begun to sell, she wants to get a New York gallery.

I said, "That'll be hard, won't it?"

"I've had some feelers," she said, in her tough way, making it clear she was not just another hopeful heading for the big city. "I'm going to be talking with people when we're back there next month. The galleries are looking for good women."

I said, "I know," and mentioned that I had friends who might be interested in buying some of her work. But after I had explained, Pamela politely allowed that possibly she was getting a bit too well-known for that level of speculation.

Then Mickey began to talk about his piece in *Penthouse* in a way that I gradually understood as a circuitous apology for aspects of it he was afraid I hadn't liked. It was necessarily slick, he said, they demanded that, but he thought he'd been able to make some interesting points. He felt funny, appearing among all that exploitation, though he thought that compared with most mass media the magazine actually had a fairly healthy sexuality, and Pamela said that even as a feminist it hadn't been all that offensive to her. I said I was sorry, but I hadn't gotten a chance to read the article.

Mickey said, "I'd be interested to know what you think when you do. You end up having to gear your work to the rag you're writing for and that gives you some interesting problems."

This afforded us an escape into a relatively safe discussion on the politics of freelance journalism, Mickey and I each excessively careful of treading on the other's turf while Pamela listened from the kitchen. Several times I had the sense we were both speaking chiefly to her, the unseen and inaudible judge. Mickey granted that one had to write "shit, pretty much" to get in anywhere that paid, and I deferred, in turn, saying that was the only way one got read, and Mickey nodded that that was true. He paid the necessary homage to the purity of my efforts, and I replied with appropriate deprecations of their irrelevance in the world.

Consequently we sat down to dinner feeling like we weren't friends anymore. The agreement not to argue left a hole too dark and deep to discuss. Pamela tried to bring it up again, but I made a polite response that I prefer to forget; Mickey offered conciliation where none was needed, and the thing died. So we gossiped a little, exposing how few friends we still had in common, and at last the conversation settled safely on Noah. Yet even here I could not help observing that in certain particulars they treated their son as they had often criticized their parents for treating them. Please, I want to take nothing away from them; they were fine parents, and he was a wonderful child, well-behaved, charming, and, of course, enormously intelligent. But certainly nothing less than brilliance was expected of him, and while he was given a light hand and much affection, Noah showed an unnerving nascent hipness, and, like his parents, he was already a very good performer.

I supposed I thought about all this because I'd been wondering what kind of mother Charlotte would make and had decided, for the vaguest reasons, that she would be strong and kind, exactly what I'd once thought Pamela would be, and which perhaps she was, though not in the way I'd expected.

Pamela was tired early, Mickey, too. He poured us each a little brandy, and now that the evening was officially over, everyone relaxed. "We never talk, anymore," Pamela said, "Do you remember how much we used to talk?"

"Our lives are different now," said Mickey. "This is something that happens in your late twenties. It's a developmental thing."

She said, "But it's not as good, Mick," and we laughed at the old nickname, lately abandoned. "It used to be so important; we talked about our lives. Now, I can't. Harold, who can I talk about composition with, or color? Morton isn't interested. . . ."

I wondered if this were for my benefit, a complaint to appease their hippie friend lest he be too depressed about his own life. I said, "Pamela, do you really want to talk about color?"

"No, of course not. I want to talk about . . . whenever we start on something it goes to business. We're artists, and all we talk about is business."

I said, "We're shy." Mickey started to object, an objection I knew I couldn't bear to hear him make, so I went on, "But it isn't worse, Pama, only different. Now we work, so we can't spend ourselves talking. Talking was our work then." Mickey nodding, yes, yes. "The trouble is, we're left alone."

"That's what I mean," she said. "It's so fucking lonely here, man. How can we stand it?"

"The weird thing," said her husband, his mood miraculously unbroken, "is how easily we do."

"But your group is still together," she said to me.

"Not for long."

"Really? I didn't know."

I had just realized it myself as we were talking. Yet now that I'd said it, I saw the end. It was too bad, but it was too late.

Pamela said, "I'm sorry. I liked that group. Where will you all go?"

I showed my palms and smiled like Shaw. We stood up. Pamela hugged me, kissed my cheek, and I hugged her back. She said, "Ouf, you squeeze hard." Once, everyone had thought Pamela could not miss.

Mickey saw me out. "It's been really good, we should do this more."

I clapped him on the shoulder reasonably well and got in the Dodge. It was finished with them. None of us wanted to go through another evening like this, and I had the old destructive urge: get rid of everything, all ties, Charlotte, too, Charlotte especially. I felt a rush of hatred for her and with it came a brilliant plan for revenge. I've forgotten it now, but these things always come back to you.

———————

17th

I begin to understand the disease of narrative: first one thing, then another. Eventually the story reaches a point where one might like it to end (a week ago, for instance, when it was pure sex), but there are all these pages left to fill, and the narrative is forever demanding more. "And then?" it asks, "And after that?" hinting at a particular development until one runs out of excuses and gives it what it wants.

"What does it want?" asks Jimmy Wax, who loves to hear me talk about these things.

"Just change . . ." I say, becoming wary (who does Jimmy report to?), "event."

"For instance?"

But is it really the story making these demands? Do I even care what happens next or only that something new continually appears to save me from the terror of boredom? When I told Charlotte not to come over the other day, it wasn't a plan or even a thought, yet now it seems part of this incessant drive for change. Change for its own sake.

I don't say it quite like that to Jimmy Wax, but he is smarter than he seems and gets the gist. He laughs and says, "So how will you keep it moving?" With that the plan I'd thought of up at Mickey's comes back to me. It is not as brilliant as I remembered, but it will work. And since Jimmy is so interested, let him be its agent.

18th/19th

In my preoccupation with Charlotte, I have failed to mention that since his editing job ended, Jimmy's always tenuous relations with the faithless Lucy have disintegrated almost to nothing. Yet three or four weeks ago, before I had even noticed this, I began dropping by his room in the hour before dinner and talking a while. There was no premeditation to these visits; they seemed to spring from the internal rhythms that govern the course of a friendship. I found him subdued, a mood of his I like, and his expressions of vague disenchantment seemed simply the usual complaint about one's life and failure, the end of his job and the imminence of rented rooms. Even after I began to sense Lucy as the real cause (Donna and Shaw both observed the change, and together we reached this surmise), I didn't question him too hard. Gradually we reestablished the rapport that my affair with Charlotte had disrupted. (Out of Lucy's sway, Jimmy was less preoccupied with virtue.)

What I am trying to understand is why I did this, and, specifically, how I had the blind foresight to put off the Lucy discussion until it was most useful. Is there an unconscious strategic faculty that guides us? In the end I did not even have to initiate the crucial conversation, and that, I believe, is the detail that will save me from detection. Who could accuse me of deviousness when Jimmy came by my room on his own last night, finally wanting to talk about Lucy? I said, "How is she?"

He offered a sickened smile, hoping to acknowledge everything by that and spare himself the torture of naming specifics. "You probably know more about it than I do."

I knew that Lucy was fucking the chief gynecology resident with an eye to an internship (my interpretation), but that didn't take much time, and since her relations with Jimmy (as with everyone) were adamantly "nonexclusive," I assumed she was just moving on and took the opportunity to taper off a relationship that wasn't going anywhere interesting. I made an uncertain gesture.

Jimmy said, "What?"

I shook my head.

He eyed me suspiciously, but let it slide. He didn't really want to know. "What about Charlotte?"

"Good question."

He smiled, "Yeah, lately things haven't seemed so, shall we say, cool with you two either." I admitted this, and Jimmy's cheerfulness returned. "What's the prob? The big J obviously."

"But not the way you think," I said. "It seems he might have something of his own going."

"Far out," said Jimmy, "where did you hear that?"

I said, "Did you know?"

He shook his head. How would he know? "What happened?"

"Just little things. One day Charlotte saw his schedule, it had him down for Tuesday night, and she remembered he'd been there on Wednesday."

"Maybe he switched with someone."

"Sure, but why? She didn't want to ask or he might get suspicious about her. The next week the schedule called for Friday, but he went on Tuesday and Friday."

"Looks bad. Charlotte does a one-and-a-half?"

"Yeah, but tuck, because there are two ways into this. Here she is . . ."

"Fucking her brains out," said Jimmy.

"With someone who's almost a friend, while he's . . ."

"With who?"

I shrugged, "Someone at work?"

"What's he on, now?"

"Ob-gyn, right?"

And I kept talking, pretending I didn't notice Jimmy's face going bad as he considered the obvious possibilities, attributing to Lucy exactly the sort of opportunism she was, in fact, displaying, though in a different, more Lucyesque, direction.

I said, "Maybe he's back with that pediatrician."

Jimmy shook his head. "He's through with her."

"Who says?"

"Lucy." Now Jimmy's attention was elsewhere. A moment later he escaped the conversation, the telephone disappeared into his room for half an hour, and thirty seconds after it had emerged he was driving off without even saying he'd be gone for dinner.

Donna said, "What's with him?"

And maybe it was only then that I thought about what I'd done. Maybe it wasn't a strategy after all, maybe none of this was, just impulses that afterward, as I sit here writing, I decide I have planned in advance. By which time, of course, it is always too late, and the thing is moving on its own.

Jimmy was too wired to keep his facts and suspicions straight. At first Lucy would think she'd been informed on, and when she realized it was a case of mistaken identity, she might even feel a certain titillation from the rumor. But the story would not hold together, particularly since to the best of her knowledge (to the best of mine) Joshua was not having an affair with anyone. So, finally, sensing me woven into the fabric somewhere, Lucy would become suspicious. She wouldn't know quite why or what about, and would decide that the only way to protect herself was to bring it all down. She would talk to Joshua; it would give her an excuse to say what she'd wanted to anyway. At first he would not understand, then he would not believe, then he would try to confirm for himself. In the end he would talk to Charlotte who would call me. I calculated that the whole process would take five days more or less.

Less than five hours later, I answered the phone, and Joshua said, "Don't you think it's time we had a talk?"

I said, "Sure."

"I'm at the hospital tonight, but it isn't busy. You can come over now."

I said, "Okay," then pictured his white coat and reconsidered. "Oh, wait," I said, "I can't tonight."

"Why? Are you seeing her?"

"Someone else. What about tomorrow?"

"Fucking punk."

I will arise and go now, and go to Innisfree, Nine bean rows will I have there, a hive for the honey-bee . . .

"I get off at six tomorrow night," he said, "meet me at . . ."

"I can't come to the city tomorrow. It'll have to be over here."

"You want me to come to Berkeley? Look, I work all day."

I said, "Me too."

"I thought you stopped at noon."

Very good. "I've changed. Let's say quarter to seven. You know The Boat on Telegraph?"

"We're having people to dinner. It'd be much easier if you—"

"Easier for you, not for me. Quarter to seven at The Boat?"

"Six-thirty."

"Fine."

I hung up, and it rang. Charlotte said, "Who was that?"

"Him."

"Oh, shit."

"What happened?"

"Can you come over?" Her voice preempted any discussion of how safe or for how long. It was after midnight.

She wore a sheer smile over her distress and was having a drink. "You want one?" I shook my head and sat across the coffee table from her. "He wants me to move out."

I said, "Well, that's what you've been talking about, isn't it?"

She nodded her thanks for this encouragement, though what she really wanted were complications.

I asked what had happened. She had gone over to the hospital about ten to have a late dinner with Joshua. When he wasn't at his station, she went to the lounge and found him with Lucy. I can picture that exactly: they sit facing each other, knee to knee, and Lucy is speaking in her precise, emphatic way while Joshua nods endlessly. They sense someone at the door and look toward Charlotte. It is obvious at once that everything has been said. Their faces merge into a single, hideous mask of righteousness. Charlotte's back is to me, so I cannot see her expression, which is just as well. Lucy leaves. Charlotte takes her chair, and in the long discussion that follows, Joshua announces that he is moving out. Charlotte says that he doesn't have to, she will, but actually there's no reason for either of them to because she's pretty much through with me. He doesn't believe this, or, suddenly sensing his power, chooses not to. He says she evidently needs some time to straighten things out, and he's going to give it to her. He is odious, yes, but who can blame him?

I said, "So what did you tell him?"

"About what?"

"Us."

"I said I loved you."

"Why?"

"It was such a relief telling the truth."

"Fuck the truth."

"You asked."

"No, I'm sorry, I was just thinking how he must have . . . I guess it is, I guess it's better to know."

She nodded.

"But then you said it was over with me."

"I said it had gotten confused. It has, hasn't it? I love you, but I never know what you want."

"Me either."

She smiled. "And I still love him."

"But he doesn't believe that."

"He says I'm afraid to admit I've stopped. Maybe he's right. He said he'd been thinking of leaving me for two months."

He probably had, but at the same time he must have thought, why did this guy have to come along and bother our lives? Things were okay. Why didn't he leave us alone? Fuck somebody else. There are lots of women. A man works hard, he thought, then he comes home, and his wife has betrayed him. Why do they betray us?

"What's the matter, Harold?"

I looked up. "What?"

"You look so sad."

I felt crazy, not sad. "Did he tell you about the pediatrician?"

"Who?"

"Some doctor. He was fucking the shit out of her at the beginning of the summer."

"Yes."

"He told you?"

She nodded.

"What did you think?"

"I'm numb." Her face had gone slack. "Then I decided he was right. I should move out." But somehow this resolve had weakened in the meantime, and now she was afraid. "Where will I go?"

I said, "If worse comes to worst . . ." as it inevitably would. It was all coming down now, falling out of the sky. My strategic faculty had abandoned me, and I had no idea where my desires lay, much less my interests. So I just kept Charlotte talking while I tried to think of what to say, realizing, finally, that she needed the whole big pitch, Christ in the wilderness, Zarathustra on the mountain. I referred, in passing, to a predictable array of ideas from Buddhist to Lawrentian, suffered momentary bouts of nausea whenever I made the mistake of listening to myself, but rallied each time and eventually brought it all back home telling her, "You are . . . you have always feared . . . you know that you never will until you, . . ." drawing on that sure sense of the terror that plagues us all—until my intensity, the late hour and high drama of the night conspired to give the words a prophetic force. Gradually her life became an awesome project, and for a moment it was 1967 again when the only issue of consequence was the progression of one's soul.

I said, "Move out."

"I will."

I took off her underpants and ate her as she sat on the couch, then entered her, thinking, as I came, that all my efforts had produced exactly this, a solid, respectable, but distinctly non-revolutionary orgasm. This cost, this pleasure, a bad bargain, but precisely human; the name of our life was "better than nothing."

I woke about four and dressed quickly.

She said, "I want you to stay."

"In your new place."

"Why not here?"

I kissed her.

Fog had come in from the sea, spilled over Twin Peaks, blanketed Market Street and the Mission, filled the crevices of Noe Valley. Above it the freeways hung suspended in the orange glow of the city like paths of fate leading to Oakland or San Jose. But the pavement had a will of its own and eased the car east onto Route 80 toward Oakland.

Now I had her and could do what I wanted with her. Her commitment to moving out would call his bluff, he would relent and keep her. At a moment of doubt she would jump for a safe place, Joshua. On and on on 80, seven miles of bridge, then dark warehouses at the foot of Berkeley. But now that I had her I couldn't think of what to do. She was mine, therefore I was Joshua. I did not want to be Joshua.

19th still/again

Now it is madness without letup.

I got home, lay on the bed still dressed and observed that my body stank. It was six-thirty in the morning, and I considered getting up to take a shower, but in the long run that entire range of things seemed too much trouble; I didn't have time for it, I didn't have time for anything. So I turned my head away from the offending armpit, the phone rang, and it was nine-fifteen. Charlotte wanted to know if she could stay here while she looked for a place. It was impossible with Joshua. He'd come home for an hour and been horrible; she'd thought he was going to hit her. She had to leave immediately. Was it all right to come here?

"Yes, of course."

"It would only be for a few days."

"All right."

"I wouldn't do this if it weren't necessary."

Yes, yes, yes, yes, anything, just don't plead. All right?
"Harold?"

"I'm sorry. I'm tired. I'll talk to you later."

"I'm going to look for places today."

"Good. I think Pamela's sister might have an extra
room."

"I don't know, she's a little. . . ."

"Okay, sure, that's all right. I'll call you later."

I had no appetite. I brought coffee to the desk and stared
out the window in stupefied, speed-shot exhaustion. She
called again in the early afternoon. They'd talked at lunch
and things were better. I was not to worry, she wouldn't
have to stay here. I told her I hadn't worried. She said
Joshua was even getting to like the idea; they both needed
some space. I was suspicious of that, but said nothing.

At six-fifteen I washed my face and walked up to The
Boat. I remembered that Joshua had drunk white wine that
first evening at Lucy's, so I ordered a half-liter of Chablis
and asked Joyce to bring two glasses. She filled each, I
tasted mine and put it down. For a moment I forgot why I
was there and who I was meeting. Joshua came through the
door, looked into the room across the hall, then over here.
He had lost weight, yet seemed bigger than ever, like a ravaged bear. He said, "Hello," sat down and took a sip. Joyce
asked if he wanted anything. He looked at her a moment,
said no, and she went away. He said, "Should we go outside?"

"If you want."

He considered this, but shook his head. "I'd like to know
why you didn't tell me."

"Tell you what?"

"That you were in love with my fucking wife," this attracting some attention from neighboring tables.

The windows were dark, and it was raining a little. "Why should I have told you?"

"It's what a man does," he said.

"Is it what you do?"

"I would."

"You would? You don't know what you're talking about."

In another situation he would have hit me. Part of his brain was saying, pound the fucker, but that was impossible here and, once he started thinking about it, much too complicated. He had no idea how to be as angry as he felt.

I said, "I guess I thought it was up to her to say anything."

"Charlotte. Up to Charlotte," he said. "Say her name."

"Charlotte."

"You're such an asshole, Harold, and you don't even know it."

"Sure I know it. Look, tell me how you'd say it."

He said, "I wouldn't have to."

"I know."

"What's that mean?"

"Nothing. I forget." I had no idea what we were talking about. "Do you want anything else?"

After considerable thought he said, "Why did you do this?"

I didn't answer.

He refilled his glass, drank it and refilled. He said, "It doesn't matter. If it hadn't been you it would have been somebody else. You think this is about you, don't you? It's got nothing to do with you." He looked up to see what I would say, but I was just watching him. He looked back at the wine glass and sighed. "I remember one time telling her, 'Do what you like.' This was about a guy she was attracted to, 'Fuck him if you want.' I said it because I wanted to be like that, was trying not to be so. . . . But of course she thought it meant I didn't care.''

I said, ''She knew you cared.''

''And I was wrong, I wasn't like that. I fucked some, I know you know it, but it was stupid, and it was always shitty.'' He laughed at himself. ''This hippie shit, it's ruined my life.'' He was silent, turning the glass so the liquid rolled around the bowl. Finally he looked up as if surprised I was still there and said, ''Go away.''

I put two dollars on the table and went outside where it was dark and he could fight if he wanted. I walked slowly and was not afraid. Perhaps I knew he wouldn't follow and therefore hoped he would. Then I heard myself say aloud to the empty street, ''Okay, fine, go ahead,'' and I had no idea what it meant.

The phone was ringing again or still, and it seemed I no longer slept, only dozed briefly between calls. I said, ''What time is it?''

''Very early,'' she said. ''Can you come get me?''

''What happened?''

''Nothing special,'' but when she described the evening, it had obviously been quite special.

Joshua was silent through dinner save for flashes of scorn and sullen contempt, and the dinner guests, glancing nervously at each other, seized the first exit line and were gone by nine-fifteen. Then Charlotte waited for him to talk, but for half an hour he stalked through the house on contrived errands until, running out of things to do, he finally came face to face with the most infuriating face of all. Her eyes offered sympathy, but he knew this was a pretense and a lie, that they were already gone, withdrawing and moving out on their own, even as they appeared to extend themselves toward him. That hurt too much.

Joshua did not really know what he was doing until he saw that monochromatic flash that always accompanied his acts of passion; then, with his arm already whipping forward and his weight shifting from rear foot to front, he became aware of the owl. It was solid Steuben crystal, about three pounds, and had been a gift to Charlotte from her father just before he died. Consciousness came too late to arrest the throw, the glass bird was already slipping from his fingers, but he thought that if he held onto it an instant longer he might alter the direction of its flight from faceward to floorward and in that manner avert consequences he was not prepared to consider. He grabbed his knee. In the moment before it hurt he thought, "a wise owl" and pictured the blue owl who had perched on the potato chip packages of his boyhood. Then there was a nauseating sheet of pain within which appeared one dot of an emotion that he identified as love. Having struck the floor, the owl had caromed off a table leg and come back at him. The dot of love widened and inside it appeared a circle of pain, and within this one of rage, then another of love, then one more of something else, then another.

Unscathed, Charlotte sat weeping too miserably to comfort him, though she must have known that nothing comforted him so well as her tears. The owl lay on its side as if sleeping; refracted light spread out like a peacock's tail on the carpet behind it. Joshua held up one arm like a policeman gently stopping traffic, telling Charlotte not to approach him though she was not trying to. He flexed the knee and put weight on it, walked tentatively to the window and back. The limp had passed to him. The moment of fear that had terminated in the knee left her feeling ravaged. She saw that he was afraid that she was seeing him afraid. He tested the knee professionally, feeling the bones with his fingers; he tried to think of other things to show her.

She took off her clothes in the bathroom and ran the shower. Joshua's hunger returned; he got out the remains of dinner, opened a beer and lay on the bed watching television. There was nothing like a shower; the heat touched a point behind her sternum and released something, the water made a sound on her skull. Beer, food, television in bed, Charlotte in the shower, these pleasures were emptied of the eternity that usually gave them weight. He found himself drinking from his glass in sync with a man on television drinking beer from another glass. The glasses came down almost at the same moment, and a popping sound on his lips corresponded to the slight sigh of the man in the commercial. The water stopped, surprising her, though she had turned it off herself. She was through with both of them. A man on television talked about his divorce and how much he loved his new girlfriend. This reminded a woman of something about herself. The two dinner guests had just finished discussing the strange behavior of their hosts. The bathroom went on being the bathroom. Without looking, Joshua reached behind him and felt around in the air for a place to put the plate and glass, and when he finally looked over his shoulder saw he'd been missing the table by two feet. He heard the bathroom door and said, "What happens now?"

He had changed, or the change of circumstance made him different. He would never be as strong again, and never strong enough. Her first husband, they would say in later years, was a doctor of some kind, wasn't he, an ordinary man. He held her back for a time, then one day she'd outgrown him, and it was over. Who thought that? It was over.

Then it became still weirder. Gradually all objects and actions acquired a numbness, occurred at a distance, slowly. It was impossible. By the time he got back from the kitchen, she was out of the towel, into her nightshirt, under the covers. The woman on television sang about a love affair that had gone wrong and which the people didn't have the energy to fix. He was sure Charlotte did not appreciate the poignance of this. Everything was impossible; even as hope rose, impossibility knocked it off its feet. The owl had not moved. The same man drank the same beer and liked it just as much. Her eyes were closed. He brushed his teeth and turned off the television, turned off the big light, got into bed, turned off the small light, turned to her, she put her arms around him, it was impossible.

She was silent. He would have preferred a confession that she didn't care. Car lights climbed the wall, turned and ran obliquely across the ceiling. How was it possible that it was impossible? And how could it happen so silently? Like the water going off. His penis was small and hard. This was nothing, it couldn't be the end, the end had to be something.

December 4

She got home today around four, fixed herself a pot of tea and smoked a cigarette. Obviously a bad mood, but I was not supposed to ask. Wrong, I was supposed to ask anyway.

She said, "I looked at a couple of places."

I nodded.

"They were horrible."

"You fix a place up."

"I know. The streets didn't even have trees."

"So what now?"

She glanced at me, then back down at the tea.

"You look some more?"

"I guess."

"You mean no."

"I don't know. You don't have to do it."

"I've done it."

"You have a place with other people."

"So find a place with other people."

"I don't know anyone."

"You don't know anyone?"

"Who lives like that. Who'd want someone else."

"Then what are you going to do?"

She made a movement telling me to stop.

"I think it would be a mistake for you to move from one man to another."

She nodded. "I'm going to have to look for a job, too. That'll be just as bad."

"Worse."

December 5

It is not her fault. This is not her fault. Please do not blame her for this.

_____

10th

I want to know exactly when I began to hate her. I look through these entries for the moment and the cause, but there is nothing conclusive. It might have been the day she moved in, and, as she stood here with her suitcases, I saw the first proprietary glance she gave this room. Or possibly it began earlier and was spread out over her slow desertion of Joshua; I resent her for the pain she caused him and the weakness implied by such an arbitrary shift of affection. And even in the first moment of that first evening at Lucy's I now think I saw the germ of it; I've never liked people who play up to children.

But was there really an instant in which the feeling crystallized, or is this just another effect searching for its cause? Perhaps my hatred isn't an effect of anything, but a timeless truth beyond causality. Perhaps I've always hated Charlotte, long before I even heard Jimmy's phrase, and hid it from myself until now, as I hear her laughing several rooms away, I can hide it no longer. If there is an instant, it is this one.

Still, this is rather a cerebral moment, and as I would like something more picturesque, I will use the morning two weeks ago when I drove to San Francisco to get her. She had awakened early, put the owl back on the mantel and called me. When I hesitated, she said, "Harold, don't desert me now." Her car was in the shop.

I hung up, the phone rang again, and it was my father. I said, "Not now, Manny. Let me call you later."

I drove across the Bay Bridge with the dawn traffic, a milky sun dissolving in the mirror, my flesh in puttied clumps, and the last roller coaster of speed rolling along my bones on iron wheels. The gas tank was full, I had my checkbook and a couple credit cards, and the eternal question asked itself, "Why not?" Why not just drive on past the exit and keep going south: Mexico, Paraguay, infinity? Leave everything.

And even as I was failing to explain why not, the car took the Army Street off ramp and headed on its own toward Diamond Heights. The morning was gray and moist and seemed, itself, to contain the terror that was only in my heart. I would glance at a street number, calculate the distance to go and assure myself that somehow in these eighteen blocks an event would occur to save me from the consequences of everything I had done. As I got closer I clung to each delay, tried to miss lights and failed, hoped I might forget the street, the address, that Charlotte would have fallen ill and been quarantined. Failing all this I would get it together somehow, park the car, sit a minute, then walk slowly up the wooden steps to the front door, composing myself as I climbed. I needed some space of my own, come to think of it.

However, as I rounded the corner, there she was waiting at the curb with her suitcases, and I was not going to have room to sit, or think, or wait, or walk. She was right up the block, growing larger inversely to the square of the distance between us. So without giving it much thought I spun the wheel hard to the left, stood on the accelerator, and the Dodge leapt the curb spreading an instant remake of "A Place in the Sun" all over the ice plant.

Only kidding. I considered that, checked around for witnesses, recalled the inexorable apprehension of all hit-and-run drivers on the television shows of my youth and arrived, finally, at this image. Freeze frame: the hood ornament of the Dodge has just made contact with Charlotte's thigh-length sweater, and there can no longer be any doubt about my intentions; a millisecond into the future her insides will be outside, but in this motionless instant our eyes meet and let us imagine the impossible, that she understands why. My question is, does she forgive me? And she answers, of course she does, since what could be more excruciating. I parked.

She held me, searched my face with troubled eyes, held me again. She knew. I kissed her and let her tongue into my mouth. I became conscious of the engine running and communicated a vague urgency (neighbors, Joshua), we put her suitcases in the trunk and drove back to Berkeley. She wanted to fuck right away, but I had to shower first.

It might have been then, but who cares if it was? And what good would it do me to know? Apparently it has gone on for some time, for I am already adept at gauging her moods to determine what fraction of my disapproval I may show. At lunch today I noticed the false smile she uses to disguise and announce that she is unhappy, and when I asked what was wrong, heard in my voice the impatience which, seen on my face, would have explained the smile. I was overcome with shame and disgust, and this must have altered my expression, for Charlotte's quickly changed, too. Now she looked at me tenderly, as if my self-loathing proved the affection she had doubted, and her smile, a very different one, said, yes, I feel it, too, isn't it good?

For example: Around the dinner table we argue about films and their politics while Charlotte, her face struggling like an eager freshman's, listens hard but cannot understand. It isn't that we are especially profound or subtle or that our private language is difficult to follow. She simply cannot hear. The words are opaque blocks of sound without sequence or meaning, and she will seize one phrase and grapple with it until, by the time she's figured it out, the sentences have rolled on past her, leaving this understanding worthless.

Last night it was a comedy, a great favorite of hers, she particularly liked the man with the puffy cheeks, his funny voice, the way his eyes moved, he was perfect. Other aspects of the film had escaped her, however; the political for one.

"Political?" said Charlotte.

Donna said, "They don't talk about class."

"Class, my ass," said Jimmy Wax. "She hasn't even seen it. This is Shaw's routine."

Donna said, "Hey, fuck you."

"That is a shitty thing to say," said Shaw.

"I take it back."

Charlotte said, "What do politics have to do with it, anyway," and looked at me. "I thought it was just funny for itself."

Jimmy said, "It is. You don't need to understand this stuff to enjoy the movie."

"Bullshit. What you're doing is . . ." Donna stopped to get a light off Shaw's cigarette. "What the fuck is that called?"

Charlotte said, "I loved it, and I didn't even think about that."

". . . naturalizing history."

"No, Charlotte's right," Shaw said gently, "most of the jokes work without knowing the politics, and we're all taught to think, 'It's just a comedy,' because—"

"I said I thought it was just funny."

"This isn't a criticism of you, Charlotte. Everyone's taught the same thing. That's why you have to remind yourself of the political context. You see what I'm saying?"

She nodded.

"Otherwise you end up with morons like Jimmy who think art's great, but politics is too hard."

"Politics is no fun," Jimmy whined.

It was time to go. Charlotte ran upstairs to change her shoes, and we waited in the hall, Shaw going on about Barthes and Althrusser until he saw Jimmy stifling laughter and said, "What's so funny?"

"You're so intellectual."

Shaw ripped open the door, "Asshole," and went out on the porch. Jimmy giggled. Shaw said, "Why don't you go see what happened to her."

She was lying diagonally across the bed, cleaning dirt from under her nails with a paper clip. She said, "You go ahead."

"What is it?"

"I don't want you to miss the movie."

"Tell me."

"Everything."

I stepped into the hall and told them to go on, came back and sat beside her. We listened to their conversation make its way up the block. She said, "What's happening, Harold?"

I shook my head.

"Everything's been different since I moved in. I don't think they want me here."

I did not have the strength for this, but I tried to pull things together. "It isn't that," I rubbed her neck, and though it wasn't time for sex, we would flee to it soon enough if we didn't think of something more appropriate. "What does this have to do with what happened at dinner?"

"You're all different from me. You like talking about things that way."

"What way?"

"You know. I feel like I don't belong."

"What do you mean?"

"Do you want me to leave, Harold?"

"Leave?"

"Because I can. I'll stay at a hotel. I don't care . . ."

"Come here." I pulled her head toward my shoulder. She offered momentary resistance, then yielded, burrowing into the crook of my neck, arms around my waist.

———————

10th

Charlotte has no job, and I work at home. Three or four times each morning, therefore, she slips into the room for something she needs. She never lingers hoping to start a conversation, and she closes the door carefully as she goes out. When I stalk through the house in frustration, I come upon her sitting in some sunny corner. She looks up, smiles, and I select a response.

She believes she assists me with her little ministrations, preparing lunch, keeping the room tidy to provide an orderly environment for my thoughts, asking if I need stationery supplies. Meanwhile, this disaster continues unmitigated, and I am incapable of work. Today she bought me a quart of Irish whiskey, suggesting I might like to keep it in a desk drawer for a nip now and then. What is going on? I wish I could believe she were mocking me; this would be less humiliating if it were deliberate.

But at night it seems possible. The moment the light is out we turn toward each other, and the problems vanish. So we do not talk or have much in common that way. We know each other differently, more deeply, perhaps. Coming into her, even more than climax, is the movement which completes my day. For a moment all I want to do is lie still there; then arousal or convention disturbs the balance, and we turn from each other into the privacy of orgasm. It is as if we met only in the dark. In the daylight we are strangers.

_____

14th

I was reading through these entries yesterday, when she came in looking for a pair of scissors. She nodded at the notebook. "Do you write about me in there?"

"About everything." She didn't like that. "Here," I held it out to her.

"You wouldn't write what you wanted if you thought I'd read it."

"That's probably true."

"Then I won't."

Charlotte resents my work. She denies this, claims I only say it because it pleases me, but how else can I explain the look on her face the first morning I told her she had to be out of the room by nine? At that moment she decided I was running away from her into the work, and that this notebook had become the concrete form of my withdrawal.

There may be some truth in that. In fact, I often wonder if writing itself isn't the real problem. I might say in the notebook that Charlotte "depresses" me, yet when I look at the entry a day or a minute later it seems I could have as easily (and honestly) written "delights" or "intrigues" instead. Yet I am most often moved to words by melancholy, rage or fear, and, worse, the act of writing is itself splenetic. The further I look into a subject, the more language seeks out its vile and petty crevices. It is like a horse who knows the way home; it always comes here. Nevertheless, these entries seem to me a maze through whose elaborate circuitry there is a path, among countless, back to Charlotte herself. I have lost her among the words, but am convinced I can find the original within the one I have invented.

So I try tenderness. I come up behind her and put a hand on her stomach. She holds my arm between her shoulder and cheek without the delirious affection that makes me want to slaughter her. I participate willingly in the discourse of kisses, touches and looks that are her constant chatter. We fall into warm silences reminiscent of those first afternoons. This is a discipline for me. We're going away for a few days after Christmas.

December 18

Having considered the options, we decided that while Charlotte ponders graduate school, she should try to find a job somewhere in the art world, and to that end she has been systematically calling every museum and gallery in the area, following up leads and using the contacts she made as an investor. She averages an interview a day, and is rejected each time. Often, through some failure of the application form, she does not learn until she walks into the office that she lacks the necessary qualifications, then she must stand up almost before she has finished sitting down and drive home. More commonly, the discussion runs an awkward fifteen or twenty minutes at which point it is determined that Charlotte's experience is not sufficiently official. Here and there she has been put on waiting lists.

By now she has difficulty finding places to call or the nerve to pick up the receiver and dial. She drinks ten cups of tea a day; she has hives; she has a cold; she is gaining weight; she dislikes social situations, particularly when they involve meeting new people; she spends an increasing proportion of her time in our room. I have noticed that she catches herself now as she speaks, stops, starts again, attempts to rearrange her thoughts and syntax and finally blurts out a mass of words that lies formless in the middle of the room. Then she looks at me to see if sense can be made of them, and I refuse to help. This, she admits later, is the only thing I can conscionably do, but it wounds her bitterly at the time since it "seems to imply" that I am dissociating myself from her.

Such dissociation would leave her completely alone, as

154

Charlotte has apparently dropped or been dropped by all her friends. Lucy sided with Joshua; presumably the others have as well. Yet when I've asked about this, I've gotten the odd feeling there really weren't other friends. There were names, usually in pairs, with whom an evening was occasionally passed, but none of these seems to have been particularly intimate. She mentioned one woman with whom she'd worked for a while, but they haven't seen each other in over a year.

The only person not to desert her is her husband. They talk on the phone every few days and go out for a meal once a week. He keeps asking what went wrong, and Charlotte tries to explain the analysis I have given her. Joshua anticipates reconciliation; she is vague. She would like to hold open that possibility (things are sufficiently horrible here), but she would consider that duplicitous and, in a sense, a betrayal of me.

Why she should be so honorable in my behalf, I cannot say, for certainly I am no source of joy. I try, of course, but lately the problems of the day have begun to follow us even into bed, and often I have difficulty finding ways of seeing Charlotte in which she is still desirable. I try to focus on her hair; I have always loved her hair, yet now it has dried and faded and is frequently twisted against the pillow in a tangle suggesting the troubles of her life. Lying half under her, I open one eye, and a rosy parabola of flesh rises through the field of vision. Instead of desire, I feel obligation. I kiss her and try to lose myself in the kiss. Her flesh is salty, the underside of her tongue slick with saliva. I close my eyes, but they are already shut. I concentrate on the mass of hair, the hum of flesh, the dense odor of cunt, the gradual obliteration of light until there are eight seconds of desperate darkness, and then we sleep.

21st

Mickey and Pamela gave a party the other night for Martha Winklemann who has just returned from a year in Italy. Word preceded her through various correspondents that while the rest of us withdrew into the gardening and carpentry of our decline, Martha was living in a Maoist collective in Bologna doing dissertation research on the local Communist party. She had published an article in a radical British journal with another due in the spring. Hearing all this, Charlotte decided not to go, but her timidity so infuriated me that I bullied her into coming anyway.

It was a mistake. Though less awesome than reported, Martha was belligerent as ever and looking very good with her coarse hair chopped short and brushed back from her forehead like a sheaf of rusted iron. Once, when it grazed my arm, I wanted to grab a fistful and squeeze it into a wire ball. Instead, I glanced at Charlotte just in time to see her head turning away.

I thought, fuck it, and went into the hall where I found Pamela sitting alone on the steps, chalk white and sweating. "I'm sick," she said, "I've been throwing up. Could you drive me to my sister's? I'd ask Mickey, but he wouldn't want to leave the guests. Wait here, I'll just get Noah."

It was a twenty minute round trip, and when I got back, an extremely long and handsome young man had stretched out on the arm of Charlotte's chair and was talking to her about the end of painting. I took a seat and listened. I could not tell how much he knew; he had a careless, fluent manner in which things were obvious (the more obscure, the more obvious), and it was taken for granted that "we" (he and Char-

156

lotte) knew all about it (had read, seen and thought the same things) while the rest of "them" persisted in missing the point. After a while I tapped on Charlotte's empty glass, she handed it to me and smiled. The young man and I took an instantaneous mutual dislike, obliging me, against better judgment, to toss a question of the "but isn't it true that?" genre at his theories of visual art. Garth (I learned the name later) slammed it over the Coca-Cola sign on the roof in left-center, intimating, as he circled the bases, that my question had its origins in the depths of envy, not to mention the shadows of ignorance. Had it really? I smiled cryptically and, under cover of a useless and private joke, fled.

I looked for Martha, but she had gone chasing after a German woman with whom she was later found on the floor of Noah's room. Fringes of the party threatened orgy. Mickey renewed his pursuit of Donna, but she told him to forget it, and he ended up out on the cold deck talking business with Barry Mann and a millionaire Barry had brought over from Marin County. I drank steadily, in my fashion, but stayed away from the drugs into which Shaw and Jimmy had vanished hours ago. Ab Potter stood at the edge of the dancing and tipped an imaginary hat when he saw me. I shouted over the music, "Divine, man, I'll have it for you by the first of the year."

Ab nodded, "Whenever. No big hurry."

I said, "No, really, I'm on it."

He laughed.

Charlotte and Garth reappeared at discreet intervals, wound ever deeper into their conversation, the space between them closing slowly. Perhaps I did smoke a little grass, intersected in my meanderings the path of a remarkable joint, the legendary roach of a roach of a roach, I believe, whose effect was to so rearrange the floor plan of the place that I forgot this was a house I knew well and instead

set off exploring its unknown reaches. Then I was in a hall-
way kissing a mouth that tasted faintly of aluminum. It was
Imogene (honey hair and nail polish) from the Tolman animal labs gushing from a silver dress and asking why I hadn't
called her. I said I'd forgotten where she worked, but she
didn't believe that. "A paranoid like you?" she said skepti-
cally. "I thought you never forgot."

"I'm going out of town next week," I told her, "I'll call
you when I get back."

"No, you won't," she said. "Take me home now."

"I'm with somebody."

"Take us both."

I laughed. "She wouldn't like that."

"I bet she deserves it."

It seemed that Imogene had more lip than there was room
for in the circle of her mouth, causing a slight and erotic
buckle. Her fingers were feathery, and I held her breast in
the shadow of a telephone alcove. She broke away with a
laugh, "Come in here," she said.

She opened the door to a small dark room full of people,
yet silent save a faint ringing, as though a large bell had been
struck several minutes before. A space opened in the center
of the floor, we knelt there, and a smiling black man filled a
foil pipe with opium and held a match under the bowl while
Imogene smoked. She passed the pipe to me, and the match
followed it. I got one good hit, another less good, then the
mixture went out. I sat back. Everything had changed without changing. The interior of the opium was marked by a
mellifluous clarity that gradually teased out of people and
objects all those qualities usually called subjective. These,
then, became palpable physical attributes, as objective as
color or shape, and there were no longer any interiors except
those of the opium and the room, which were now perfectly
congruent. (If one left the room, would he break away from

the influence of the drug or would he expand its circumference?) There was a warm, comradely rapport among us, nothing cliquish, just a pleasant sense of being in it together, which I would be loath to attribute solely to the drug. I regretted having to leave as much as they regretted my going, though of course that was my prerogative, and no one said anything to stop me. I picked my way over the bodies, edged through the door and went into the bathroom across the hall.

Someone was there already, a man about forty-five or fifty with a fleshy face and big, broken eyes I couldn't see into. He was too old and guarded to figure out, yet he was unmistakably myself, extrapolated twenty years to that unknown wisdom already recognizable as what I would learn. His face had given up the effort of being handsome, and the good looks of its youth were displaced downward into a fine gut that I hoisted about with an awkward grace. I rather liked myself this way; I evidently ate well, I appeared to retain my humor, sex was still an issue if already a problem. But I could not, from this side of the mirror, see through the face on that side to whatever it knew that would change me into it. And the eyes were careful with this knowledge, as though in direct contrast to their youthful selves they rationed energy with an appreciation of its finitude and kept what they knew to themselves. I ran a hand over the thick cheeks, turned off the light and went out.

Charlotte was gone and so was Garth. Shaw, sitting on the floor with a boyish woman, said that Jimmy had taken the Dodge, but he didn't know if Charlotte had left with him. Donna had met someone. I was not worried, or, if so, only abstractly. The crystalline opium air accompanied me on the walk home, and I wondered was I still inside the opium, or was it inside me? Was the question a Klein bottle? Should I change my name to Klein, or was I too short for that, like the incredible shrinking man who climbed through the wire screening back into the garden? The night was beautiful, was it not?

She was in our bed, alone, reading. I was astonished how happy I was to see her there. I said, "I thought you'd gone home with him."

A rueful smile, "I thought you'd left me."

We kissed, her breasts pressing against my chest.

"He was interesting," she finally admitted, "but I'm not attracted to that type." I was excited that she felt it necessary to lie. Right after I had come into her she said, "Harold, let's not do this to each other again."

23rd

I always know when it is Joshua calling; a peculiar tone permeates the house, and I suddenly find myself liking Charlotte more. When it rang this evening I was cooking. Immediately I turned down the flame and strolled into the hall. Charlotte was at the top of the stairs, just around the turn, sounding cheerful and optimistic. I busied myself in the coat closet.

She was saying, "No, I'm fine . . . Yes, really . . . Well, nothing's ever perfect . . . No . . . No, I can't tell you when, I have no idea, maybe never. . . . I didn't say that, I said . . . You said . . . Well, anything's possible. . . ."

I should have left them alone, but I couldn't. How she must have wanted to tell him the truth, that her situation here was desperate, yet through some excess of pride or loyalty or wish to spare him false hope, she went on blandly pretending everything was all right.

Donna came through the door and looked at me strangely as I stood transfixed, half within the shadow of the closet, a coat in one hand, the other in its pocket, but not moving.

Charlotte said, "I told you it wasn't that, not directly. . . . That was fine. . . . Yes, of course, I did, you know that. . . . Not every time, but. . . . Well, who doesn't have problems? . . . Sure, he does, you should. . . ."

Donna said, "Jesus Christ," threw her coat at me and went down the hall to the kitchen. I heard a beer open, her feet going into the living room, and a second later the piano was banging out all possibility of hearing Charlotte. Well, I am without shame, that was established long ago.

In any case, these conversations with Joshua generally take this form and have become redundant. After a recent one, however, she announced that she had one hundred dollars to her name. She has decided not to accept any more of his money, and she cannot borrow from her mother since her mother is being kept in the dark about the split. Her rent is fifty-seven, groceries are only twelve a week, but she has expensive habits, particularly alcohol, and she is used to buying what she wants. I have been reluctant to lend her money, only because it would make the inevitable separation one step more complicated. But the day she asked for fifty dollars I received a check for three hundred from my father (something about estate taxes), and I gave Charlotte the whole thing, telling myself it was an hourglass that would run out the moment we'd finished with each other.

25th

"It's Christmas," said Manny, "I wonder if you could give us a sign of your coming."

"I can't get away right now."

"When do you think?"

"How is she?"

"Holding on, but these things can turn quickly."

"Maybe a month."

"A month?" Like the grunt of a wounded animal. "You said Christmas."

"I have to finish up something here."

A tightening silence as Manny wondered cynically what I conceivably could be doing of any such urgency. "Listen," trying his always futile tough tactics, "I want you to come now."

"I'm not coming now," I said. "I'm going away for a couple days. I'll call you after the first."

———————

December 29

The moment we got here Charlotte said, "It's perfect, isn't it? And quiet for your work."

Quiet? How can it be quiet with the money chattering away day and night saying, "And you? . . ." The owners of this house are friends of Joshua's parents; he's a proctologist, she's a sculptor, and they are everywhere in evidence. There is enough food for a wedding, enough liquor for a wake, a closetful of sheets and towels, hundred-dollar lamps, thousand-dollar couches, walls of books, walls of glass, redwood decks (and this is just their weekend place). A small study juts seaward from the top of the house like a ship's bridge, and I am supposed to write up there, looking out at the shifting plates of slate that comprise the end-of-the-year ocean.

Naturally I raved. Charlotte had gone to such lengths to get it, calling the owners (who'd offered it repeatedly to Joshua and her), enduring their hesitation (stories of the split had reached them), resisting their suggestion that she and Joshua go off together to "get back in touch," lying (always hard for Charlotte) that she needed some time alone.

Later, no doubt, proctologist and sculptor discussed this with each other. He snorted at Charlotte's "writer," announcing that he'd never thought the girl was good enough for the Cobin boy. But the sculptor understood that her husband had had a fatherly sort of crush on Charlotte and now felt betrayed; she'd always preferred the girl, herself, finding Charlotte warmer than Joshua.

"A woman's not like a man, Ben," she said in conclusion.

"As a physician," said Ben, "I don't think I need to be told. I just don't like the idea of this writer screwing her up at our place."

"But she's going there alone."

"Oh, horseshit," the proctologist said.

But, in fact, Ben's specific fear has yet to be fulfilled. We have spent three nights in their enormous bed with the ocean view carefully discussing our troubled relations. Throughout I have been a paragon of patience, explaining with stunning clarity why it is impossible for us to live together. I feel as though I have never understood anything as well as I understand this, yet though I can convince Charlotte of each individual point, she resists their cumulative conclusion. Her final refutation consists of flinging her face into the pillow and crying, "I can't stand hearing you say that. How did it change? I used to make you happy. You said I made you happy, and now I depress you, I depress you." And she cannot stop saying the words, as though repetition might wear them out. "Why should being cheerful depress you?"

"But you've been miserable yourself since you moved in."

"Because it's been different between us. I haven't been able to relax."

"That's what I can't stand; you're becoming like me."

"I know."

"You're not spontaneous anymore. You catch yourself and hesitate."

"I know."

"I can see you listening to yourself as you talk and wondering how you sound. You're afraid you sound stupid and are making a fool of yourself. You think everyone wants you to stop talking. You can't . . ."

A silent shriek. She bends the pillow over her face and shudders. "It's that I've been looking for a job, and the house, and things being bad with us. It's a bad period, it's the worst period of my life, but it'll be all right when I get some money. Not having money is terrible."

"What if it isn't just money?"

"What?"

"Maybe there's a way you'll always be if you're living with me."

"Why do you like to think that?"

"I don't like to, I—"

"You always say it. Do you want me to leave? Do you want me to move out?"

"I'm just trying to suggest—"

"You liked the way I was at first, didn't you?"

I nod.

"I'm going to be like that again."

I nod again.

"Don't say that. It's true, I am." And her smile searches for the confidence that first attracted me. So I will have to wait until she knows, too; then we can nod like chess players agreeing to a draw and stop the clocks.

From the deck of the study I watched her walk along the beach. She wore white pants and a gray sweater, and the wind snapped her dark hair against her face. When she saw me watching I thought she would wave, but she just stared up as I stared down. A minute later she continued walking, and I came in to write.

January 8

A good week. We have gone our separate directions, then looked for each other in the dark. I thought about calling Imogene, but it seemed unimportant. Charlotte stills me, completes me and carries me down to that imperceptible flow at the bottom of life. The window on my right, the bed on my left and this desk between them comprise a sufficient world.

12th

Charlotte is in the kitchen peeling apples. It is a little past four, and with the dwindling light she feels happier. The mornings, when everyone is busy (even Shaw now), are the worst for her. She tries to go through the motions of looking for work, but usually Jimmy ties up the phone (calling about jobs for himself) and occasionally, worse, he leaves it free. When things get very bad, she takes her car and drives around absolutely nowhere for a couple of hours. Sometimes she pulls over to the side of the road and cries. She never tells anyone about this.

But at lunch it gets better, people sit around talking, and she feels less crushed by empty time. In the afternoon she lets herself run errands and lately has gotten in the habit of making dessert almost every day, whether it is her turn to cook or not. They even tease her, "What's for dessert, Charlotte?" and she likes that. She has a secret fantasy that they are all really her children (adopted) and that, as with desserts, it is she who brings the sweetness to their lives. She smiles as she works, dreaming of this without thinking it.

She finishes slicing the apples, throws away the peels and cores. She hears me on the stairs and does not even recognize herself flinch against the anticipated contact. When I come into the kitchen she cannot tell exactly what is bothering me, but then she says to herself, "He is about to do something. Is he going to tell me now?" She has felt something brewing for a couple of days, and now her heart slams against her chest in panic. However, I just look in the refrigerator, ruffle her hair and go out of the room again. She feels relief almost to weeping and a sudden hope that everything is all right. The front door opens and closes. She says, "Harold? . . ." She decides I must have gone up the street to the Park & Shop.

She makes a lattice crust on top of the pie and puts it in the oven. She goes into the living room and glances up the street to see if I am coming, then gets out one of her art books and looks at the pictures. She tries to pay attention to the formal elements Shaw talked about (perspective as an expression of psychological depth, color symbolism), but that is too boring. She just likes looking at the pictures. It depresses her to realize this, and she closes the book as the gate clanks.

However it is Donna who comes bounding through the door. Donna says, "Hi," starts to put a record on the stereo, then hesitates. "Is it okay if I play this?"

Charlotte smiles, "Sure," and Donna smiles back. Charlotte likes Donna better now, not as much as she likes Jimmy, but much more than Shaw who always makes her angry no matter how nice he tries to be.

Donna says, "You want a drink?"

And Charlotte says, "Yes," so fast that Donna laughs, and Charlotte laughs at herself. She looks out the window again. It is getting dark. The sky over the Bay is stormy, and she worries that I'll get wet.

They have just fixed two drinks when Jimmy comes in and says, "Hey, me too." Then the three of them sit in the living room, Jimmy talking about friends from film school who have moved to Los Angeles and wondering if he should, too, and Donna bitching that the guys in her band never let her solo enough. Charlotte feels euphoric and a little high. She wishes the world would freeze like this, and they could sit together forever in the early evening having drinks.

The timer goes off. She comes into the kitchen, takes out

167

the pie, puts in a casserole. The front door opens, and she hears me greeting Jimmy and Donna. I sound so cheerful, and she does not recognize her heart sink, but when I enter the kitchen (flushed, happy and wringing wet; exactly the opposite of how I'd left) Charlotte receives my kiss with misgivings. She says, "Where did you go?" wishing she could have resisted asking.

"For a walk."

It has only been forty-five minutes, but Charlotte is afraid. A walk where? Whom did I see? She cannot humiliate herself with further questions, but she can feel the truth like acid in her muscles. I am already out in the living room talking and drinking with the others, but Charlotte remains in the kitchen in silent, shrieking rage, pounding the counter top with her flat palms to keep from going mad.

———————

15th

Last night when I got out of the car, I started toward the theater, then stopped and waited for Charlotte to catch up. But I felt stupid waiting. Why should we walk together, I thought, why not apart? What does it mean to be "with" someone? Where did we get that idea? Yet there I was, standing and waiting, and when she caught up, we walked together in silence, and that was supposed to be better than walking separately. I have the suspicion that everything I do makes as little sense as this.

———————

18th

What hypocrisy. Since my futile visit to Imogene's laboratory the other afternoon (she was out sick; they wouldn't give me her home number), it is all I think about. Idiotically I squander the days asking myself whether or not I should call her, when the only reasonable question is, will I? If I will (and I will), I ought to do it and shut up. But no, I prefer agonizing over it for hours, telling myself I'm trying to resist the temptation.

My father again.

———————

Sunday

When we got in this evening, she went directly up to the room and closed the door. I pretended not to notice and sat in the kitchen talking with Donna and Shaw, deliberately making jokes so Charlotte would hear us laughing. After an hour I came blithely upstairs and jumped into bed as if everything were perfect.

As I picked up my book, she closed hers. I found my place, then glanced over as if I sensed something on her mind. She said, "Do you remember when we first sat down in the theater?"

I said, "Yes."

"Do you remember that I was talking to you?"

I didn't, but I nodded.

169

"Right in the middle, Shaw asked you a question, and you turned around to him and ignored me from then on."

I said, "I thought you were finished."

"I was in the middle of a sentence. And you didn't just answer him, you talked for five minutes. You didn't turn back until the movie started."

I said, "No, what happened was, after I answered him I turned back to you," I turned toward her now, "and you said nothing, so I turned back to Shaw."

"I didn't say anything because you weren't listening."

"You were looking straight ahead. You ignored me."

"I was angry by then."

Then? What then? Weren't we making this all up? "Why didn't you say you were angry?"

She shook her head.

I said, "I thought you were finished."

"I was in the middle of a sentence." She looked sullen. "I don't like being ignored."

"Being? Is it something I do often?"

"You've done it before. You did it when we went to that dinner."

"At Barry Mann's? Is it possible you were particularly sensitive that night? As I recall you were upset, you were jealous of that woman. In that sort of mood people tend to take offense pretty easily. When something like that happens, it's because of problems between the people, it's something we both did."

"What did I do?"

"That night?"

"Any time."

"You withdrew. The minute we got there you hid in a corner of the couch and looked depressed. It was a drag on everyone."

"I didn't think you noticed."

"Noticed! I was humiliated."

She was close to tears. "Then why didn't you do something?"

"Do I ask you to look after me?"

"If we were with my friends, I—"

"But we're never with your friends, and even if we were . . ."

Throughout this conversation and others like it, the twinheaded gooseneck lamp by which Charlotte had been reading threw a mottled light on the wall above us, revealing each imperfection in the plaster and accentuating the elliptical water stains. It gave to the entire room an unnerving aura of decay. Cold air blew through the cracked window, and even in the night I could see the glittering branches of the tall hedge bend and bend like old Jewish heads nodding over some sad wisdom. How sick I was of melancholy and sympathy.

"You'd never have turned away from Donna or Shaw like that."

"That's ridiculous. What are you saying?"

"That I hate this."

"Do you?"

She nodded, crying. "I hate it, I hate it."

"Well, so do I, my little bitch."

Her crying turned to sobs and became a kind of retching. Finally I held her, she grew quiet, we made love.

———————

Friday

Imogene's line was busy. I took it for a sign: I wasn't meant to get through. And since, having placed the call I'd proved my courage, I was free to observe the sign and not place a second. If Charlotte came home now, that would settle it.

On the other hand, what if it weren't a sign, but a test? Impulse could get you started, but perseverance required more. One proved nothing.

Still busy.

Charlotte had been gone half an hour and might return at any moment. Donna came naked into the hall and went into the bathroom. The shower ran. There were no signs, only tests. I called again. The front gate clanked just as we were making arrangements, and I hung up an instant before Charlotte opened the door. Already I regret the call and what it commits me to, but fortunately there is no undoing that now.

Saturday

At three o'clock I will stretch and say something about going for a walk. Charlotte will look up with a shy smile, indicate her willingness to accompany me, and I will reply with a brooding look and a slow gathering of my troubles about my shoulders. She would like to be invited, yet cannot help admiring the manly self-possession that excludes her. Interesting that I use a characteristic Charlotte loves to

172

wound her while I suppress my natural need of company for this effect.

I will walk out the door. She will see the top of my head crossing the bottom of the window and feel a twinge of loneliness that masquerades as compassion for me. She will not observe the slightest difference between this and countless similar scenes.

Ready?

———————

Saturday, midnight

If I had gone home when the Deaf School bells rang five, it might have passed for a long walk. I pulled back the curtains and looked out on a red, marble evening veined with blue. A silent black bicycle tilted almost flat as it flicked around the corner. Imogene sat up and said, "Well, you have things to do, and so have I." Certainly there was no reason to stay, yet something was intriguing.

Naked, Imogene seemed smaller, hardly more than a handful, and the taste of metal was everywhere on her, like a perfumed poison in all the private places a tongue might look. And to what end? To kill men, of course. Me in particular. Why? Because we were vain and foolish; here he was, stepping out on his old lady, but when he tasted poison on a woman's skin, he was afraid to admit he was afraid, thought she'd see how fucked up he was, so he drank his death instead. What else? She liked watching them choose to die. I kissed her. She laughed at me. A warm, dead river ran into my brain.

The illuminated clock dial said ten to six. Pinned above the bed, two life-size foil skeletons, one silver and one gold, caught what little light was left in the sky and floated out from the wall on a breeze of undetermined origin. I asked her where she'd gotten them.

"In Cuernavaca," she said, "on the Day of the Dead."

"How hip can you get? What were you drinking, strychnine?"

"Cocaine, darling, straight from Peru." It was easy to picture: Imogene on the slopes of Popocatepetl snorting it through thousand-peso notes with rich boys from Mexico City. Afterwards they go to the family estates in Morelos, then into Cuernavaca at night. "They adored me," said Imogene.

I said, "What's Mexico like?"

"It's the end of the earth. It will blow your brains away." And as if in confirmation, the silver skeleton shuffled its feet in an impromptu soft-shoe while the gold skeleton held still.

"I have to go," I said.

"So do I."

"This is going to be difficult."

"With your little chickie? But you love it."

"Why do you say that?"

"Look at you." I looked, and it was true. She laughed. "Are you hungry? Listen to me." I put my ear on her stomach, and the bells said that it was seven times too late to go home. I imagined Charlotte in the green chair, staring at the television; the seventh ring cracked her heart, and I felt so tenderly for her it was as if she limped again. Imogene's face floated in the silvery gold of her hair, and the skeletons glinted as they moved.

When I got home, all four of them were sitting in the blue glaze of the late show. Shaw gave me a wry look and Donna said hello, but Charlotte and Jimmy didn't even turn from the screen. I stood behind them for a few minutes, letting their accusations bounce harmlessly away, then came up here and began to write.

Charlotte has just entered the room. She looks at me, but says nothing. She cannot decide what to do. She turns and begins to undress, folding her clothes and placing them carefully on the chair. This indicates that she is good; it is too bad her mother isn't here to appreciate it. Now she is in bed, and the desk lamp stretches lovely shadows across her face and throat, reminding me of Murnau's *Tabu*. In a moment I will undress and climb in beside her, and she will let me do anything. I could break her like an ear of corn if I wanted.

All will now despise me.

31st

This afternoon we went up to Ho Chi Minh Park and lay on the grass reading the *New York Times* like any normal couple on a Sunday. Yet it all seemed incongruous. Emmanuel Raab, who was probably reading the same newspaper at that moment, had never, I was fairly sure, spent Saturday night in the arms of anyone but my mother. And I realized, as I failed to comprehend a single sentence of the paper, that I had long since implicitly believed that the reading of one's Sunday *Times* depended on innumerable factors, the fidelity of one's Saturday nights among them. This was apparently untrue. One could do anything he wanted and still read the *Times*. I had noticed when I bought the paper at the bookstore that nobody asked for credentials or letters of recommendation; a dollar thirty-five was all they wanted.

Someone said, "Hello," out of the sun.

Charlotte sat up quickly. She said, "Harold, you remember Garth."

I certainly did. I stuck out my hand and smiled. Give Garth credit, he made no pretense of an interest in me, and as soon as he had led the conversation back to private and technical realms, I read the paper, looked at the sky, and eventually even got up and wandered off out of earshot, acting as though I wanted to get a better look at the tennis players. I kept my back toward them in what seemed to me a rather impressive display of detachment. Then I heard Charlotte say my name, I turned, and she beckoned to me with her head. She had fallen backwards from her sitting position and now reclined propped on both elbows. Garth sat beside her, a couple of inches too close, I thought, his big knees pointing up into the air.

He said, "You don't mind, do you?"

I looked at Charlotte.

"Garth was asking if we had an exclusive relationship."

No fucking shit. For the life of me, I couldn't think of the right answer. I said, "Nothing official."

Charlotte said, "I think I mind."

Garth laughed, pushing the hair out of his eyes, and said, "Why?"

"I just don't do that very well." She said it coldly, but of course she knew how attractive that made her, the edge of reserve.

Garth gave a good-natured and faintly patronizing grunt of understanding. "No offense, I hope."

"None at all."

"No," said Charlotte. We all smiled idiotically, and he left.

Charlotte and I were silent for some time, each of us turning through our sections of the paper. "You know," I said, "in a way that might be a good idea." She shook her head.

"But if we both did it . . ." She flinched; it had not been confirmed until now. ". . . If we both did it, it might help things betwee us."

"You can do what you want," she said, "I'm not like that."

"But actually you are. I mean how did we get started?" She looked at me with loathing. "And it's obvious you're attracted to him."

"I'm not."

"All right, but if you weren't involved with anyone else, it's possible you could be."

"He's too pushy."

"Actually, I thought he did this pretty well."

"But I'd already told him I didn't want to."

"At the party?"

"Yes, and he called up the other day."

"Far out."

"Why?"

"Because you didn't tell me."

"I said no."

"Yeah, I know; that's not what I mean."

"What do you mean?"

I mean . . . I mean . . . I mean far out.

February 3

Is it that I don't love her, or that I can't stand her loving me?

4th

Perfect. This is exactly what should have happened; I'm only surprised it took so long. Returning, today, from a completely innocent walk, I found Charlotte slunking about the house, and when I asked what it was, she said she hadn't known what was "going on" with me and, afraid to bring it up, had opened this notebook and read the previous entry. Luckily, that gave her such a blow that she'd looked no farther. For some reason I remembered what I'd written and was able to explain the "actual feelings" behind the text. Charlotte learned that the question in question was more about me than about her and reflected a general state of alienation rather than specific doubts about a particular relationship. This made her no happier, but at least it confused her unhappiness into an anesthetized silence. Yet even as I shaped my reassurances to fit the shifting surface of her fear, I could not understand why I didn't simply tell the truth.

What is a liar? It is someone with a secret he keeps even from himself, and he invents delicious surrogate secrets to help disguise the original. He pretends to hidden alcoholism, homosexuality, madness; he imagines himself a sadist, an idiot, loveless and unloved, a child. But deep in his heart, no, deeper than that, he knows that these, too, are lies and disguises concealing something else.

Test him. Discover his false secret (he will blurt it out at the first opportunity), then take it away from him. Say, "Don't be silly, you have those feelings like anyone else, but that doesn't make you _____." This is most reasonable

178

reassurance, eminently correct, yet he will resist it with the farthest fetched arguments and cling to his "horrible secret" like a thing beloved. It is his briar patch, the fear he knows, and not willingly will he be driven to others he has not yet learned to love.

6th

I have seen the skeletons dance again and heard the bells. I got home at five this morning, and when I walked into the room, she jumped out of bed and began smashing me with her little fists. Wonderful, I felt a flash of the old love. Then her anger snapped off into tears, and I lost interest. I tried to seem sympathetic, but found myself snorting with repressed laughter and finally had to run from the room to keep from roaring hysterically at the sight of her. Admittedly this is a disease.

February 12

Manny called during dinner, wanted to know if I'd decided yet. I said, "No."

"You're not coming?"

"I haven't decided."

He nodded. "I hope she isn't dead by the time you do."

"How's your father?"

"Not bad. He'd like to see you, too."

I was weary with hunting and fain would lie down.

"Why do you hate us so much?"

I said, "I don't hate you." I hated him completely. "I'll give you a call."

We hung up. A moment later it rang again, and he said, "You know I'll pay the plane fare."

I said, "I know."

He said, "Okay, see you, buddy."

My grandmother's oil-colored curls lie on the hospital pillow case, and she watches my grandfather, fumbling with consciousness like bad radio reception, shuffle in on Manny's arm and sit beside her bed. She says, "Jacob," making the *j* a *y*, and when he laughs she realizes it has been years since she's called him anything but Jack. Not that it matters. There isn't much left of either one at this point, Jacob or Jack. Her husband has vacated this body that is going to outlive hers by years. He only needs a name now and then (it doesn't matter which), his hand held, a face to look at, and her only consolation is that she will not have to be the one henceforward; a nurse will be hired, the children on weekends.

He says, "How are you?"

"Not so bad," she says and smiles so Manny can see she knows different.

Jack says, "Good, good," in a reedy way that makes her realize she's misjudged him. He can still tell when she lies, and he must know what this lie means. For a moment, then, the three of them know it together, and she likes that. But Jack can't hold on to it, hasn't enough left to keep it specific, so it dissolves into a general depression that settles over him like a drug. He is gone, and she is going, and finally he will go, and they will be over except for the children who don't really mark anything.

She says, "How about you?" He looks up and grins, pleased with her for asking. She has always resented this innocence of his, acting as if everything were fine, but for once she is too tired to take it away from him. She just smiles back, glancing again at her son to make sure someone else acknowledges the truth.

Manny answers with a small shrug, an ironic smile. Manny, too, is weary with hunting. It is almost ten at night, and he hasn't eaten since lunch. He would like a drink. For weeks and months he has had the task of looking after his parents. His sister, his wife, his sons, they leave it all to him. Manny does not realize how he keeps them from helping, how he declines their offers before they are made. How he . . .

Finally he says goodnight and walks alone through the hospital parking garage. A pretty woman passes. His mouth is dry. The leather seat of his car. The lights on Broad Street. The radio. The night. The river winding toward his home. Manny knows that he will die. Not tonight, but some day.

Valentine's Day

Nothing is too much for her.

Charlotte has finally been persuaded to go out with Garth, but don't ask how; there are deeds too terrible to tell. I helped her decide what to wear. I sat on the toilet and talked with her while she brushed her teeth and combed her hair, and when she was beautiful I saw to it that she put the diaphragm and cream in her purse. Naturally, I encouraged her to stay with him, suggesting I would sleep with Imogene.

But instead I have remained home alone to observe the long night of her not returning. It is one of those rare pleasures that never dull with repetition, and in the waiting one always discovers some peculiar truth. Tonight, for example, I learned that it is not Charlotte's absence I mind (that is even pleasant), rather it is her persistent not returning that has gradually become intolerable.

Of course, the process has been slow. At mid-evening, ten o'clock, say, I would merely glance up from my book now and then, note that she was still out and feel a slight twinge. It was a mixture of pain and annoyance, but there was that ironic chaser (who was doing what to whom?) to wash it down with, and I returned to my reading.

By eleven-thirty things had begun to elongate. I had trouble following the sentences. The number of separate moments in which Charlotte failed to open the front door was increasing, and the pain intensified proportionally. Finally I became angry with her. She should have known better than to take me at my word. I really wanted her to come back, this was just a test. (Or a sign.) I plotted my revenge; I would do the same to her. I recalled that I'd done it already, that she believed I was doing it now. So what? It was different when I did it; I never cared about Imogene. I laughed at this. I laughed at everything I thought. I was glad she was gone.

But the three hundred seconds between midnight and five after contained, theoretically, an infinite number of Charlotte's not-returnings. Some of these were experienced directly, others by generalization, and it was difficult to say which hurt more. Then a strange phenomenon occurred, for as the pain passed a certain threshold and frequency, it began to seem independent of the event, and I had to remind myself that this had anything to do with Charlotte.

Now, when there is no longer a reasonable hour at which to expect her, the pain breaks free of specifics altogether and becomes pure time. It isn't the hands of the clock that cause it anymore, and it isn't Charlotte. Time passes, and it hurts, and the soundless uncreaking of the front gate, the car doors that come to nothing, do not matter at all.

15th

She got home at seven, still wet from him, and I was inside her a minute later. Some fucks have a theme, and this one's was the rediscovery of lost love. With pure faces and classical movements, we searched through the muck of the intervening months for that clear place we occupied in the fall. The premise was that it still existed, like Atlantis, preserved in the crevices of her cunt and that my cock was a long, silver submarine with which we searched for it. We groaned and swooned as though in ecstasy we had gotten there, but we hadn't; sex was simply sex, and I couldn't tell if it was good or bad, preoccupied as I was by everything it was not.

I woke at eleven to the familiar panic that the morning was going by without me. A red Coca-Cola truck pulled up at the Park & Shop, and the store manager signed the invoice as the driver unloaded the cases. Light flooded the street. The tall hedge swayed against the window, and there was something so poignant in its movements, the branches pushing down and rising, the lacquered leaves scattering an applause of sunlight, that it seemed to say it all.

Charlotte still slept, and in her tranquil face I saw that I would never make anything of these feelings while I was with her. She wanted us to inhabit a world of sex, food, drink, drugs and the open air. She could not understand why I didn't have time for that and had to work instead. For all her dislike of Berkeley, Charlotte belonged in this city of defeat and daily pleasures. Frankly, only a special sort of person could make those branches say it all, and Charlotte was not the sort of person that sort of person lived with.

I dressed and walked up to The Boat for coffee. Barry Mann was out on the patio reading *Variety,* and he said to me, "Are you sick of this place, yet?" meaning Berkeley.

I said, "Yeah, I think finally I am."

"I'm taking my script down to LA next week."

"And do what?"

"Pound on doors," he said, "What else?"

"This is another porno thing?"

"In a way," said Barry, "but it's political, too. There's a whole economic analysis. The logo's going to be, *Tits and Class.* What do you think?"

"I think you ought to rip off Aeschylus and call it *Hard Corestia.*"

"Too arty. I don't want to sound like an intellectual."

"Don't worry."

"I just want to make a very straight presentation: story, appeal, market. Then I say, all right, for eighty thousand I can rent the equipment, buy stock, pay tech up front, get a low-budget classification from the union and all other salaries deferred. I shoot in nine days, bring it on schedule, at budget. They see numbers, a distribution stategy, here is the break-even point . . . very clear, very professional."

"Barry, who's going to give you eighty thousand dollars?"

"Man, we made *Orgy on Mars* for under ten, and it's

done one-oh-five in eighteen months. The figures are right here.'' He shook the pages of *Variety*. ''On paper, I'm a great investment. I'm telling you, Harold, you ought to come down there.''

''LA?''

''Knock out a couple of scripts and make the rounds. What are you doing now?''

''Writing.''

''Writing what?''

''It's hard to describe.''

''A script?''

''No, I don't know, maybe it could be. Nothing commercial.''

''Art.''

''Lay off.''

''Look, we're living in the dying stages of monopoly capitalism, right? What does Marx tell you? There's a drying up of investment opportunities, particularly in the domestic market. At the same time you've got a lot of fairly big money hanging around looking for tax shelters. An independent film is ideal: high risk, stories of fabulous returns, otherwise a write-off. How can you lose?''

''There must be a way.''

''What's the alternative? Hanging out in Berkeley the rest of your life being hip?''

''That's true.''

''Seriously, man, I worry about you sometimes. You got to get going.''

''Yeah, you're right. In fact I have to go right now.'' I stood up. ''How long will you be down there?''

''However long it takes. Come down and take a look.''

''I would, but I've got to go east for a while. Maybe when I get back.''

Barry tipped his cup at me and drank it down.

Back on the street it was the same dangerous day that had been there when I woke. The word TEXACO turned slowly around to say TEXACO, turned and said TEXACO again. Two men with briefcases got into an Oldsmobile. Someone had surveyed the street, a crew had spread gravel, poured asphalt and smoothed it down. A municipal agency had contracted for this work, authorizing the expenditure through a vote of the city council. The contracting company was a subsidiary of a large, publicly owned corporation that employed, no doubt, thousands of workers. The average workman went home in the evening. Lights burned behind the curtains of his house. After dinner he sat down in front of the NFL and poured himself a drink. He fell asleep in the third quarter. Wednesday nights he fucked his second wife. His first kid was in college becoming . . . I don't know, a CPA or something.

And I was nothing. Nothing in the morning and still nothing in the afternoon except the panic of being nothing. I lay on the bed, and fear alchemized my blood to mercury; my body shook with cold until it splintered like a broken thermometer, the chair flipped over, and that irresistible laxative emptied my bowels. Pound on doors.

Charlotte knocked softly, came in and smiled at me. I tried to convince her I was simply tired, but there is no fooling Charlotte when it comes to feelings. She sat on the bed and stroked my forehead, traditional folk remedy for the blues, not the country, city or electric blues, but the weekday, washday, daytime-TV blues; the powder, not the midnight blues.

"You've been working too hard," she said.

"I haven't done a thing in weeks."

"Look how tense you are."

Wandering the Avenue, nauseous in bookstores, I was supposed to have been working too hard? Could she possibly know how much I hated her knowing me? I put an arm around her waist, realizing too late how she would take it. She permitted the advances she'd requested, but the simplest kiss was a lie. Now even my erection insulted me. I kept expecting it to crumble and explain what I could not, but it just stood there like a column holding up a roof that had fallen in. Once inside her, erect but unaroused, I tried to stimulate myself with thoughts of Donna or Imogene's poisonous mouth. But these did not get me off, so I thought about Charlotte with other men, with Garth or the Texaco mechanic, or with someone wandering in off the street who, finding her sprawled across the bed one drowsy afternoon, has her all creamy before she realizes it isn't me.

She fell asleep, but I could not. I was afraid to get up and afraid I'd lie there indefinitely. If it had been dark I could have left the room, but in the daylight of a Wednesday . . . I could have written Barry's script better than he had, and my own script would be better still. I thought of going over to the desk and starting work on it right away. Then I would have a lot of money. Not that money mattered, but it did. I knew that I had to stop thinking this way. Go through it, I advised myself, not around it. I came over here, opened this and wrote this. It's a bit excessive; things aren't this bad.

Manny again. And again. Messages accumulate by the phone. Manny wakes me in the morning and puts me to bed at night. "Harold when? . . . Harold, please. . . . Harold, my son, it is getting late. . . ." By now he has Jimmy and Donna and even Charlotte asking me every other day when I am going home.

I can hardly answer, only sit in crushed silence, finally muttering into the phone, "Not now. Not just yet. There is something I have to do first."

"What could be so important?" he wants to know.

How could I explain? How could he understand? ''A small transaction, Manny, a little corporal divestiture.''

''What are you talking about? Are you being funny?''

''I'll call you.''

But isn't it obvious that whatever it is he wants from me, whatever Charlotte wants, or Jimmy, or I want from my fucking self, that I simply can't do it.

Then the phone rings. It will be Manny, of course, calm this time. Or pleading. Or angry. It rings again. And worse even than disappointing him is the realization that I am numb to his pain. I don't care. And since there is no one else in the house right now, I just let it keep ringing.

20th

She is moving out. I have to help take her things over to Lucy's. More later.

Later

We were in bed last night, and she asked, ''Where do you think we'll be a year from now?''

I lay in the dark thinking that I would be dead if I were still with her in a year or a month or even a minute. I said, ''I think we will be in different solar systems.''

She laughed.

I said, ''I'm going to sleep with Imogene tomorrow night. You want to make it three?''

She stopped laughing. "Why do you try to hurt me?"

I said, "Because you're a wimp, and the only thing wimps are good for is punching around."

A long silence, then, "Do you want me to leave?"

And finally I said, "Yes." Yes. Yes. Yes. Yes. Leave. Go away. Go home. It was all I could do to keep from leaping out of bed in delight, stuffing her things in a suitcase and chucking it and her out the window. Yes. Yes.

She said, "I knew I would have to be the one to say it."

Did she want a medal? I would gladly give her one.

She said, "You're a coward, you disgust me."

Touché! Touché!

I also repulsed her. However, she also loved me and wanted me to change my mind. She wept. She screamed. She was sullen. She was stoical. She clawed at her face with her fingernails. She. . . .

But the time has come to cease and desist. There is no end to this voice. I have looked for it in these pages, but now the notebook is almost finished, only a little bit to go, and I have realized I could go on exploring in this direction forever without reaching the end. It is the infinity of the infinitesimal. Death would come first. Instead I will shut up. No one wants to hear any more, I do not want to write anymore. Only what is necessary to fill these last pages. That is a duty. Then I will go home to Manny.

In the morning we packed her things, drove them over to Lucy's, and I came back alone.

23rd

Now the proper order of the world has been restored. Lucy comes again to visit Jimmy (though not to sleep with him) and brings the gossip. Last night she told us that Charlotte and Joshua have been seeing each other "now and then" on a "trial basis." Ridiculous. How many now-and-thens fit in three days? Why didn't she just move back into the old house, hang her clothes in the closet and start dinner?

Lucy also mentioned Charlotte's rundown on me, "masochistic," "sees the worst in everything," as well as Joshua's assessment of why *it* didn't last: "He lacks substance." Lucy smiled, I smiled, I loved it. But this morning it enrages me to imagine Charlotte walking around with her opinions of my character. Shouldn't we have some authority over who is allowed to think about us?

25th

We fucked and talked, and I atoned for unnamed crimes by not enjoying my climax and by eating Charlotte to ecstasy as of old.

Of Joshua, she said, "We've seen each other a few times. I'd forgotten how much we had in common," etcetera. Then, "And last time we made it together." Betrayal: I'd taught her to say fucked, and already it was "made it together." I nodded and put on a thoughtful expression. For a moment I thought she wanted me to say it was all right, but she went on, "It's not the same."

"As what?"

Her look included the bed and us. I nodded again. That's when I ate her. She still came like a train, but who wants to live with a train? I thought this one would be different, but they are always the same, even to my thinking they will be different. There was a tenderness in the beginning. Does it hurt you, Charlotte, knowing it was like all the others, more or less?

We went out to dinner. Jimmy, Donna and Shaw were making something, but neither of us wanted to eat with them. Charlotte expected to stay the night, but I sent her home. She did not want to leave. I cannot bring myself to tell how I made her go. I mentioned Imogene, other things. That was enough, and she fled. I called Imogene, but she wasn't there. I went to bed. My stomach hurt.

March 2

Today it was my mother calling; they're "giving" Grandma Flora two weeks. If I want to see her . . . The change of interrogators (which is Mutt and which Jeff?) had the textbook effect: I cracked and agreed to fly east on Saturday, kiss her, catch the funeral and get back here by the middle of the month. Frances shrugged at my timetable. She is beyond pain.

Then, in the mail, this:

Dear Harold,

I want you to know I think you've been incredibly

191

shitty to me. I'm beginning to understand why we couldn't live together (though I doubt I have the same reasons as you) and how that precipitated some of what happened before I left. But it doesn't excuse the way you've treated me since then. For a long time, I've defended you, first to Joshua and Lucy, and lately against a part of myself that was getting angrier and angrier, by saying, "he doesn't want to be like that," "he can't help it," "he suffers too." But none of these explanations did anything with my anger, and I realize now that you like suffering, you want to be like that, and you can help it as much as anyone. You're a prick, Harold, a premeditating, an incorrigible prick. I sentence you to life as Harold Raab, sentence suspended.

When you asked me at dinner last night if I'd been living at the house the day Pamela's sister overdosed, I realized how little attention you'd ever paid to me. I was too embarrassed to think of this then, but do you remember who found her behind the storage shed? And who called the ambulance while the rest of you ran around the house hiding the drugs? When I asked why you couldn't remember my being there, you got so defensive, your voice shot up so high and squeaky the way it does when you're frightened, that for the first time I saw how ugly you could be. And I liked that. It was how you always made me feel.

Not always.

Since then I've remembered other times when you were ugly and I hadn't been able to see it. Why couldn't I see it? Isn't that what you'd ask? I couldn't see it, prick, because I'd been won over (read: intimidated and blinded) by this shit about your tortured soul, so that what was really ugliness, I saw as a kind of pain

that made you noble. And writing this, I'm so humiliated all over again that I feel like smashing your face
in. But then I realize it was my fault as much as yours.
It also didn't do the relationship much good; if we'd
gotten past that right away, who knows?

The point is I don't want to see you anymore. We
could drag it out for a few more weeks to its horrible
end, but that would hurt both of us and spoil the tender
feelings we still have for each other. I'll miss you, miss
talking to you, touching you, hearing you laugh, but I
have to do this before I can change in ways that have
become necessary to me.

Harold, I hope you find some real happiness and
don't, as you put it, settle for five minutes of peace of
mind every three years. You try hard, but there is
something in the way you try that botches it up. I think
if you were given a perfect happiness (perfect for you)
you would look at it and love it, and keep going over it
and talking about how great it was until you found
yourself becoming a little bored with this side of it and
discovering a slight flaw in that one, and you would
gradually seize on these aspects and become so preoccupied with them that they would come to seem the
whole thing. Then you'd decide you'd demystified it,
as that bastard Shaw says, and that you didn't like it
anymore. And when you've demystified the whole
world, Harold, what then?

I wish this meant I'd stopped loving you. I can't help
thinking that if you appreciated yourself as much as I
do . . . But why talk about it. What I've learned from
you, isn't it funny?, is that there are more important
things than love. I don't know what exactly, but I'll

193

drop you a line when I've figured it out. In the meantime, prick, please leave me alone.

Much love,

C.

P.S. Don't call either.

Dear Charlotte,

You forget only that having demystified my "perfect happiness," I would be perfectly (if but momentarily) happy.

But quibbling aside, you are right. There is something very simple and necessary that most people do without thinking that I cannot do at all. As a kid I used to think of myself as a cripple who ran, danced and did acrobatics to keep everyone from noticing that he couldn't walk like a normal person.

———————

March 4

No reply.

———————

March 4 again.

She was always saying, "Please, if you change your mind, . . ." and now that I have, she's apparently changed hers. I called Lucy's and she told me not to come over. Wouldn't give a reason. She preferred Joshua? Fine. I hung up, called the airline and made a reservation for tomorrow.

Then I drove over to San Francisco. A wind like dog's breath warmed the city, and Charlotte was packing her things. I said, "Joshua?" and she smiled, but without embarrassment. I hurt and wanted to hurt her. She had no idea what it was like inside this body, tropical tortures occurring silently. I said, "Good."

She came over and put an arm around me, but I went away. I smelled of bad nerves. "Harold."

"What?"

"Sit down."

I sat on the arm of the same chair, though she wouldn't get the reference. I put a hand in her hair without wanting to. The pain that had inhabited my stomach for days was now traveling down into the scrotum where it kept a syncopated beat. She shook my hand off. Why bother? Close the door and walk away. Leave everything. Just leave it.

I said, "Can I have a cup of tea?"

She got up to put on the water, then remembered, "You don't drink tea."

I nodded, "Yeah, well, I'd like some. Is it okay?"

"You don't feel well, do you?"

"I want you to come back, Charlotte."

She went out to the kitchen, and when I heard water run in the kettle, I followed. I said, "I didn't know until you were gone . . ."

"What are you doing?"

". . . until you were gone . . . that, Jesus, Christ, why do you make me say it?"

"I'm not making you do anything."

"Please, I want you to come with me."

She went back to the study and continued packing. Didn't she see that she was nothing? Didn't she feel herself cartwheeling in the wind? I followed, and she said, "Get out of here, Harold."

The desk leg made a shallow depression in the carpet, and within this a faint shadow circled the foot. For some reason I thought of Bob Callison, who could not stop talking once he got started; it was a disease that began with innocent remarks, then degenerated through cruelty in search of death. I hadn't seen him in a year or two; it was time to look him up. "I love you," I said.

Something struck the bone that orbits the eye. I covered the eye with my hand, and in the other one saw Charlotte breathing hard and not sure what to do next. Her face was disorganized, the features didn't know quite where to go, and in their confusion left an empty space, like an opening onto rage. It excited me to think of her so angry. I wondered what she'd thrown and looked around the floor, but couldn't find it. She went about her business. The eye did not hurt much, and I had to admire her for going that far. She'd earned the right. One free blow. *Gawain and the Green Knight.* I smiled. She swung roundhouse and caught me flat on the ear. That hurt, and the bitch landed sitting. Fuck her. Sitting. Blood puddled on her lower lip and spilled onto the white Mexican shirt she was wearing. I became preoccupied with the white field of the shirt as it was silently dotted with blood. My hand hurt. She wiped her mouth, smeared it across her eyes and into her hair; streaks of blood arched in butterfly wings from the corners of her eyes, ran down into twin streams of mucus that seeped into her mouth. Rorschach. She spat blood on the floor. She spat it on my shoe and the leg of my pants. I sat beside her, and she spat at me, but there was nothing left in her except air. Her nipples were like acorns. She said, "I don't want to."

"Yes, you do." I reached inside her underpants. "See."

"That doesn't mean that." I lifted the shirt over her head and took off the pants. She moved against my hand. She played with my penis and put it in her. She said, "This is stupid. Let me go."

"Doesn't it feel good?" She had never been so sweet.

"Yes, because I love you."

"I love it, too."

"What's the difference between loving it and loving me?"

"Time."

She laughed. "You feel good."

I said, "I do, yes."

I did what I could to make it last, but Charlotte wouldn't come, and finally, without coming myself, I was soft in her, and without meaning to, she squeezed me back into the alien air like a length of toothpaste.

"What happened?"

"Nothing." My penis was streaked with blackish blood. "It's your period."

She sat up and looked. "It shouldn't be for a couple of weeks." She lay down. "What happened?"

For a moment there I had thought she could kill me and that if she did I would love her, but that chance passed, and it was too late. I hated her, instead, totally. "It's my fault," I said.

"It wouldn't work," said Charlotte.

"Maybe we should get together once a week and go to bed."

She said, "Maybe."

"I'm going east tomorrow; come stay with me tonight."

She got dressed and went back to her packing while I continued to lie on the floor, looking at the stripes of swimming light the Venetian blinds threw against the wall and at the large figure moving back and forth across the room above me. The phone rang. She went into Lucy's bedroom to answer, and as I was now quite used to listening to her half conversations, I knew immediately that it was Joshua. She did not mention me, and talked in a normal voice about the details of moving and what they were going to do that night. It was as if their lives had already fit back together, and I was all but forgotten. They spoke (I could infer Joshua's side of the conversation as easily as I heard Charlotte's) like people who have talked together a long time and have devised, over the years, a private language in which the complex and subtle thoughts that baffle ordinary speech are communicated with a laconic ease. Now, even when they discussed mundane subjects, they were, at the same time, affirming the intimacy of that language, and the simplest remarks became acts of affection. Their lives had remingled so quickly because, in this basic way, they had not been apart. I realized that I had never had a conversation like that with Charlotte or anyone else and that although I was capable of dramatic heights, the commonplace, daily exchanges by which love is sustained and renewed had always escaped me. I did not know how to bank the passions for a slow burn; on the time scale of real love, I still came quick.

And once I had thought that, I had no idea why I'd ever wanted to interrupt the conversation occurring in the next room. I dressed quickly, slipped out the door and let the car coast halfway down the hill before I jump started and drove back to Berkeley once more.

The house was empty. It still is. Where have they gone? It doesn't matter. On the desk is this notebook, hundreds of pages pebbled with writing, the words stretching out into miles of twisted, cramped and swelling lines that try to hide their content in obliquity and hysteria.

I close the book and walk out into the hall. There is a note on the phone. It is for me:

H—

Your Dad called and said your grandmother died this afternoon. Call him. He's buying you a ticket on an eight-thirty flight tomorrow morning out of Oakland. You can pick it up at the airport. He sounded okay, but *please* call him. If I don't see you, have a good trip, under the circumstances. Love, Jimmy.

So.

Manny.

I come back into the room, pack some clothes in a suitcase. Then I remember that my flight is not until tomorrow, so I sit at the desk again, but of course now there is nothing to do. I can't really stand much more of this. I turn out the desk lamp and sit in the dark. The phone rings for a while. The Portuguese man comes home.

The front door opens. Voices enter and go down the hall into the kitchen. A minute later the piano begins to play, Donna pounding the keys with her strong little hands, warning us not to give her any shit like her brothers used to, making sure we know how tough she is. Now Shaw comes upstairs the way he does when he's going to make a "private" call, and sure enough there follows the squeaking whisper of the cord pulled taut as he takes the phone into his room and closes the door. Closes the door. That is how it has gotten around here. There is also Jimmy Wax who likes to miss dinner or even run off to Los Angeles for the weekend without telling us, lest we forget how independent he is.

Last winter, though, it was worse, despite the job. I have talked as if the job helped a lot, but it didn't. It was another hideout, like Charlotte and the house and this notebook I have almost filled. Is the house a hideout, too?

Shaw comes out of his room and hesitates in the hall. He is right outside my door, which is slightly open, but all he can see from there is the bed. He says, "H? . . ." They call me H sometimes.

From below I hear Jimmy, "Is he there?"

Shaw says, "Just the suitcase."

"What about the note?"

"It wasn't on the phone."

Shaw goes back downstairs. I smell cooking, the blue-red grease of cheap ground beef, and I can see them in the kitchen, Donna and Jimmy and Shaw, having a beer and waiting for the burgers to be done. There is nothing like that beer before dinner when you're all just hanging around. Later you'll go to a movie, the four of you, and people will say, "Oh, yeah, them, they're always here." But all that is over, so just leave it. Leave everything.

Now the dark window reflects the desk lamp, my right profile, the side of this chair. With an effort I can see past this to the houses across the street, the roofs behind them, even the three wires, black against a dark sky. Or with a different sort of effort I can look into the depths of the reflected room, the bed on the right, the dark oblong of the closet, the suitcase by the door.

The suitcase is ready to go, and I am ready to accompany it. It only requires quietly closing the door to the room, the door to the house, the metal gate. As I go out they will be eating, and if I am not careful one of them might hear the door close and say, "What was that?"

March 5

The TWA lounge is gradually filling with people for the eight-thirty flight to Chicago. From there I will connect through to Philadelphia, reaching my parents' home a little too late for dinner. They will have saved something for me however, part of a roast, no doubt, and when I arrive everyone will be in the living room having coffee and fruit. As I come through the door they will all say with rising voices, "Here he is, here he is . . .'' and there I will be.

A steward at the check-in desk flips on a microphone, and at the first crackle of electrified ambience, people stand and begin to line up at the gate. Some of us, however, remain seated, and we glance at each other to see who we are.

I have been at the airport all night. I got here by bus, had dinner in the coffee shop, then bought some magazines that I read in the main waiting room. There is a display of twenty-four clocks there, one for each time zone around the world. During the night I would wake, forget which zone I was in and jump up in a panic that the plane had left, though of course there were still hours to go.

The steward calls for families with small children first, then passengers seated in rows twenty-six through forty-eight, then the rest. They all shuffle slowly forward, trying not to appear foolish. One by one the people still sitting get up to join them, but I remain here on the plastic chair.

The fact is I do not know how to get on the plane. In Philadelphia, Manny will meet my flight, and shortly afterward telephones will be ringing all over the Bay Area. I cannot speak to my father. I cannot tell him that having missed the death it is impossible to face the funeral. That I do not know how to be there. That I do not know how to care. That everything will seem false to me, the faces, the dark clothing, the solemnity that I am sure no one, *no one* believes even for a moment, yet which I know contains its tiny truth, a truth I cannot locate.

There is a final call, then one more. The ladder rolls back from the plane, the door fits into place, and the nose swings slowly around to face the runway. The morning is dark with rain clouds, but in the lit waiting room one figure remains alone.

I cannot move. I cannot bring myself to stand and pick up my things. I think, instead, that I will stay in this chair, and I will just stay here and just stay here. Other crowds will fill the lounge, board their planes and leave me alone again. I will become like an object. No one will notice. If I begin to give off an unpleasant odor . . .

But even that is not a problem. There are no problems anymore, for at last I have come to the end of this book. It is right there in the corner where my thumb is, and all the rest is just filler to get me to the bottom of the page where there is no more room, and I can finally stop.

second
notebook

But if the monster will not shut up? If he races to the supermarket in the middle of the night to buy a fresh notebook? A notebook with horrible green covers because that is the only kind he can get at 4 A.M.? If he starts in at once with his hideous scrawl?

Monday

I have rented a room. It is on the second floor of a large house just a few blocks from where Jimmy, Donna and Shaw still live. Seventy dollars for twelve by sixteen feet, a table, a chair, a hotplate, a Murphy bed and a window overlooking the street. I have no telephone, no visitors and no mail. The other tenants are students, the new, industrious variety and, therefore, quiet. We have nodding acquaintances. The bathroom is down the hall.

Tuesday

Back to work this morning, but immediately the question arises: what now? and what then? Once there was Charlotte to give this momentum, then Manny to haunt it. Now there is just me. I wouldn't even be sure of that except that my testicles still hurt.

10th

Thought about calling Charlotte tonight, but I could see at once how that would go: a drink, a few laughs and recriminations, then for lack of a better idea we'd start pulling at each other's body. And what is the point of repeating these things we've done already? Some comfort, I guess, but that's not enough.

Around ten I introduced myself to Roger, the kid who lives downstairs, and called her from his phone. No answer. They were probably— No, don't get into that. Played two games of chess with Roger and won both; tried to lose the second, but couldn't.

Afterward I went by the house and got the Dodge. All the windows were all dark, but there were voices coming from Shaw's room. Whose?

12th

The work goes badly, or, rather, goes nowhere. Really, I ought to just stop, for what can happen now? One is always and only one. One plus one can generate all the positive integers, but one alone is simply solitude, morning to night.

The next day it is the same. Gradually the walls take on a certain mien. The placement of the table under the window, the open book lying slightly askew on the floor, every detail in the room comes to bear the stamp of, signify and replicate the tenant. The saucepan in the chair, a shoe on the sink . . . these are the horrors that tidy people avoid. Things arranged along the rectilinear scrupulously exclude personality. But those of us who are sloppy (for whom a shirt ceases to exist the moment it is taken off), we are besieged by the endless reiteration of ourselves until even the tree outside the window (its branches lit from within by a street lamp) seems almost expected, almost, by now, a cliché.

It isn't the tree stripped of "meaning" that makes me nauseous; it's meaning standing there pretending to be a tree. At least Blake saw a chorus of almighty angels among the leaves; I see only Harold Raab.

———————

Saturday

I have gonorrhea. The tube that carries sperm to the penis is enflamed where it attaches to the testicle, the weight of the testicle pulls on it, and that's what's been hurting. It's a nasty dose, the doctor said. He put me on ampicillin and said no sex, exercise or alcohol for at least a month.

Sunday

Roger has some people over this evening. A pot luck. He invited me, and I said I'd bring a salad, but I never got there. One thing led to another and that to a third. Or maybe I wasn't fit for human consumption . . . company. After an hour Roger came up and knocked, but I had turned off the light. Instead I sat in the dark eating the salad and listening to them talk.

No doubt this hurt his feelings. I'll have to think of some excuse.

Monday

Apologized to Roger. It was all right, I could tell. He did not even press me for reasons. We talked about playing chess again.

Tuesday

A definite plan: stop writing. Pretty easy to go a day or two without it, but then it's like a reflex.

Wednesday

There is nothing here, not even fear. Now when I wake up, I am alone. The walls are the walls, and the air is the air. Gradually paralysis sets in. One morning you cannot even get up. You drop the pencil. Hunger comes and goes. Your sentences are all stupid. Stupider than that and stupider than that.

Thursday

At first you think they will come and find you here on Elba and bring you back to Waterloo. (Charlotte was Russia.) So you sit and stare out to sea, or in this case out over the street, watching for ships, or in this case for one of them, Jimmy Wax, say, who will have followed the Dodge and found your lair and has come to fetch you home. He will tell you that one of the others is sick and has asked for you. Or he will notice that you are wounded and need tending. And of course none of that will happen; no one is coming; you are just here in the room.

You begin to invent pretexts for dropping by the house; you have forgotten your toothbrush, you need some extra socks, you sense the onset of disease, brain fever, say. Anything that gets you through the door will do.

But you stay here. It is not precisely clear why, and yet you must. Like a junkie kicking. Like a monk with frozen T-shirts still to dry. Like . . . But you don't really know like what, and perhaps that's why: you are here to learn why you are here and always have been. Homeopathy.

You take walks and find yourself flirting with familiar neighborhoods. Through a store window you see Pamela Marcus or the trumpet player from Donna's band. You are ravenous for any kind of contact, and like every addict you think, "Just this once." And like every good superego you answer, "Not tonight. Maybe tomorrow, but tonight leave it alone."

You go home. You go on. Solitude is a landscape into

which you penetrate ever deeper. Strange terrain is settled then left behind as stranger still stretches out ahead. Gradually Berkeley becomes a foreign city of unfamiliar streets and houses. You pass Imogene on the Avenue; she looks but doesn't see that it is you. Perhaps it isn't. The next time you will not recognize her. Perhaps it won't be.

Friday

Worked an hour and accomplished nothing. I cannot even think about it anymore. Absurd that I keep trying.

Spent the afternoon changing the transmission fluid in the Dodge. That was better. The car sounded good, and it was the first useful thing I'd done in weeks. Made meatballs and noodles. Read all evening.

March 23

Slept badly. No breakfast. No work at all.

24

Nothing

25

After lunch today I sponged off the table, then sat a minute watching the daylight on the Formica top and the chromium rim. When I looked up it was seven o'clock. The sponge was still in my hand, dry and turning stiff.

———————————

26

I have forgotten everyone. I say their names and nothing comes to mind.

———————————

27

Still, there is a sadness, vague and abstract.

———————————

28

Did nothing. Sat in the chair all day. This is just obstinance, a refusal to submit. Submit to what?

———————————

29

Evening. The room dims, and all objects shift slightly to the left. The last bits of daylight appear in vertical streaks along the closet molding, the posts of the chair, a heating grate. Gas ignites in the street lamps and burns slowly to a blue-white against the blue evening. The street is empty. A bicycle. A dog. A bus. A man. Scraps of paper. Two women.

———————

30

Evening, I watch the . . .

———————

31

When the

———————

1

———————

2

April 12th

Charlotte's in the hospital.

April 13

It was yesterday, I guess. I was out at the end of the Berkeley pier looking into the water. I don't really know how I'd gotten there. I'd been wandering around for a week in a kind of daze, just going here or there without thinking. Then yesterday I looked up and saw all these people with fishing poles and baby strollers, and I was on the pier. I felt as if I'd been crying.

I turned and saw a man leaning out over the opposite railing. I saw only his back, really, but it was bent with such stiff melancholy that I could imagine the face as well, and with that I realized it was Mickey Marcus. And though normally there was no one I would have been less anxious to see, today I felt only fondness and sympathy.

I crossed the pier and leaned on the rail beside him. For a long while he continued to stare out toward the hills of

Marin County, and when he finally sensed someone, turned and saw me, he wasn't even particularly surprised.

"Oh, Raab," he said vaguely, "when did you get back? How's Charlotte?"

I said, "Fine, fine," and asked after him.

He smiled, "I've got a problem, pal."

"What's that?"

He drummed his fingers on the rail, deciding whether to get into it. "I'm in love with somebody."

"Somebody you're not supposed to be in love with."

"That's it."

I nodded and saw Mickey's heart pushed open like a doubledoor safe. "I should have guessed."

"Hey, don't give me a hard time."

"I wasn't, I just—"

"Because I know you're an old friend of Pamela's and you don't like me much, but think how I feel."

"I do," I said. Mickey looked at me. "I know how you feel."

His features softened, and he nodded. "I guess you've got problems of your own these days."

I said, "Sure, who doesn't."

"See, I love Pama, you know that, but with this show coming up all she does is work, and there's no talking to her about anything else."

"Like about yourself."

"Like about that exactly."

"Well, you knew when you met her . . ."

"But you never really know until . . . Anyway, then I met this girl, woman really, Sybil. She does layout for the *Stone.*" He was almost apologetic. "It's an old story, huh?"

"But still a good one."

He laughed and felt better. "So how are things with Charlotte?"

I shook my head. "It's over. She's back with her old man."

"Really," said Mickey, "so fast? That's good."

"Why good?"

. "Well, it sounded like things were pretty horrible."

"Yeah, they were, but . . ." And then it occurred to me that that was not the kind of thing Mickey would say. I wasn't even sure he knew. I said, "What do you mean horrible?"

He was afraid he'd offended me. "Look, no one blames you, just that when Pamela saw her in the hospital the other day she looked awful."

"Charlotte looked awful."

"Yeah, but actually that was last week. She must have gotten better fast."

I realized I was drumming my fingers on the rail exactly as Mickey had been doing a minute before. I stopped and said, "Mickey, I haven't been around. I had no idea Charlotte was in the hospital."

"Really, man? Shit, she's been there since you went east."

"What's wrong with her?"

"I don't know exactly. Pama says it's some venereal thing."

I went back to the room. I made dinner. I was sorry she was sick, but what could I do for her? What had I done for her so far?

I woke up this morning and went through my pockets. I have fifty-one dollars and change, total assets. The airplane ticket was bought with a credit card, so I can't cash that. I am tempted to say this is all a game, but games have rules and goals, this just goes on. Still, I feel a strange excitement today, as if things that have been lying flat are now turned up on their edges again.

At noon I telephoned the hospital from Roger's room, but they wouldn't give out any information. "What is your relationship to the patient?"

"That's difficult to say."

"In that case, sir, I'm afraid—"

I hung up and called Ab Potter about the Divine piece. It turned out he'd already done it himself. "If I'd known you were going to come through, man . . ."

I said, "You have anything else? I'm tapped."

"Not right now, but I'll keep you in mind."

"Need somebody to clean up the office?"

He laughed. "There's a sandwich place around the corner here. You could get something part-time to tide you over."

I said, "Over what?" and Ab laughed again.

April 14

Charlotte said, "I thought you were in Philadelphia."

I shook my head.

"When did you get back?"

I tried to explain what had happened at the airport, but it sounded absurd.

"I don't understand."

"It doesn't matter," I said, "How are you feeling?"

"I'm all right. What about your grandmother?"

What could I say? "She died."

"But your father, wasn't he? . . ."

"I don't know. I guess he was."

"You haven't talked to him?"

"Not yet."

She turned her head away and began to cry. For herself and all the others. At first I felt moved to comfort her so she would stop, but then I could see no reason to, and after a minute she came to the end of it. She blotted her eyes with a tissue. When she took it away her face was calm, even a bit detached. "I had a tubal ligation."

"Is that serious?"

"Not really. There was a pregnancy in the fallopian tube, so they had to take the whole thing out." She shrugged.

"Whose was it?"

"Whose was what? The pregnancy? Mine." She laughed. "And who else's I don't know. Maybe yours, maybe not. What's the difference?"

"Charlotte . . ."

"And who gave me the clap, nobody knows. That's how the tube got ruined."

"That must be how I got it."

"You have it, too?" That bothered her more than her own. "I'm sorry."

"Please . . ."

"Kerner says I could've had it a year without knowing."

"A year?"

She nodded her head, almost crying. "I've been sick, Harold. I've had pain. You can't imagine it."

"Tell me."

"No."

"But it hurt?"

She nodded.

"Bad?"

She kept nodding, eyes closed, until tears ran out from beneath her lashes, and her body shook with shame and rage.

Friday

I went back to see her yesterday, then again tonight. She was uncomfortable and complaining, so half from vanity and half from irritation I tried to stimulate some rebellion in her against the disease. At first I hardly noticed what I was doing. I offered advice and little pep talks that must have sounded as pompous as a priest on sex. She smiled them away, but soon I was inadvertently taunting her, making cracks about her passivity, linking this to her present condition.

"You know, there was always, how should I put it, a certain quiescence about you, Charlotte. Very erotic in its way, but now something more up-tempo might be appropriate, eh? . . ."

She gave me a baleful look, but said nothing.

"Of course that's part of the appeal, the way you just lie there."

"Lay off, Harold."

"No, I mean . . ." I did not lay off. Yet as the words continued to leap from my mouth, I felt myself coming back to life, the juices flowed, and though I would have had trouble explaining how, there really was a fondness for Charlotte in all this. As though I was cutting fat from around the lean of my love. Well, maybe not love, but affection certainly; it grew even as I hurt her. "Actually, this has always been a problem of yours, hasn't it? Long before I—"

"Look, I'm tired, damn it. It's eleven-thirty. Why don't you go home?"

"Why don't you?"

"Christ. Who do you think you are, you asshole, Billy Graham?" She shoved the swinging table; it smacked into the window, and the water pitcher toppled over. "Get the fuck out of here, Harold. You make me sick."

"Oh, it's my fault?"

"Shit." Genuine rage. I felt a flash of the old passion and even thought about going for her. She saw this and shook her head. "Forget it."

"Not interested?"

"You're the only person I know who likes people to get angry at him. It turns you on."

"It's the mating cry of my species."

"That's not funny."

"What is it? Sad?"

At which we both burst into hysterical laughter, and I felt a warmth I hadn't known in ages.

———————

Saturday

The sick take care of the well, don't they? I walk into the room, she senses my discomfort, and before I can embarrass myself by asking, "How are you?" she volunteers the latest report. It is thorough, precise, good news and bad presented with the same easy dispassion. She anticipates awkward questions ("How long do they think you'll be here?") and answers them with a candor that, itself, allays my fears ("It depends on how I respond to the new drugs. There's been some activity . . . If we can get through the end of the week . . ."). And when I am reassured, when she has guided the conversation through a few neutral topics (the NBA playoffs, a book I had given her the last time), when, in short, she has allowed me to believe I've spent some time cheering her up, she thanks me for coming and lets me go home.

———————

Monday

She is better. Her eyes are clear, the phlegm has disappeared from her voice, and they say that if all stays well, they'll discharge her Thursday morning.

And immediately I am a little sorry. I have enjoyed these visits, and even more I've enjoyed the prospect of them, the knowledge each morning that that is waiting at the end of the day. I always go late at night (not wanting to run into people I know), and gradually it has gotten to be a habit. Even when Charlotte complains, I don't mind. One develops a tolerance after he's been alone; things that would have irritated him before become acceptable, even endearing.

Then, too, Charlotte, herself, has changed, and as the disease lifts, her whole manner seems to have altered beneath it. She is cheerful again, as when I met her, though with an almost musical detachment now. Clearly she is past thoughts of me, past Joshua as well. She talks about us both with a devastating simplicity. The marriage is hopeless; wounds have been inflicted that will not heal. She isn't fit for a relationship these days. That was why it didn't work with us. It is remarkable how clear everything has become.

"A lot of it," she says, "I learned from you."

There is pain in that remark, yet I'm flattered. More, I am relieved and delighted.

"You know what else? I got a job."

"Really?"

"You remember Stephen? The guy I was seeing for a while before you?"

"The artist."

"Yeah. I called him and said, 'Listen, can you get me work?' I'd helped him out, and he owed me something. The man who runs his gallery needs an assistant, he loves Stephen, so I'm in."

"Terrific. When do you start?"

"As soon as I get out of here."

April 21

So that is the end of the story, isn't it? And who can say if Charlotte is not better off for it all, if it wasn't, as I promised Lucy, good for her? Certainly the woman who, even today, may be starting her job at the gallery is an improvement over the one I found talking to child Harold seven months ago.

In any case, after that last visit, I decided not to see her again. I could feel the peculiar tug one gets when a life that has been bound up with one's own starts moving off in a separate direction. The gallery is a door to another world, the one to which Charlotte has always belonged. Within a year or two, I imagine, she will be living with an artist she has met at work, someone she does not even know today. He will be older, talented, but without any business sense. Charlotte will discover that she has a good one, can be even a bit ruthless at times. She will like that, and the money she

222

brings them. She will enjoy his children, too, when they visit. She will like his friends. She will have found her home.

I can see her now at a party they are giving. They live in a loft that has been done over nicely. Some new work is up, but it isn't for sale yet. These are just friends. Charlotte sits on the back of a couch talking to one of them. In her hand is a drink; the other hand is in one of the children's hair. And as she turns toward the light, I can see that she is lovelier than ever. She has aged, lines divide her face, yet these have only deepened the beauty and made it more sensuous; for now it is as if a past of men and passion were legible in the modeling of every feature. In fact, if one knew her well enough (if I were there, but I am not) he could point to each fold and imprinted pigeon's toe and name the person to whom it belonged. The tightening there beside the mouth, for instance, the unclosed parenthesis on the left side, that one is mine.

April 23

This evening, when I got home, there was a note from Roger on my door. Someone from the hospital had called and said that Charlotte was in the intensive care unit. She had asked for me and given them Roger's number, which I had left with her in case she needed it.

I got there about midnight. She was asleep, and I stood beside the bed watching her heartbeat bounce a green, electronic ball across a television screen. A bottle of clear liquid hung on a metal pole and ran down a clear tube to her arm. She opened one eye (it zigzagged mechanically like a bird's), then after some difficulty the other. She said a distant, "Hi . . ."

I said, "How are you doing?"

She tried to laugh. "Shit."

It had been Wednesday, she remembered, the day before she was supposed to go home. Now that she was well, now that the whole bloody mess was behind her, she lay there wondering where it had all come from, the pregnancy and the infection. Whose child had drowned in a tube constricted by what disease, spilling bacteria that came from where? The child was Harold's or Garth's, and the disease was probably from Stephen via that little girl she saw him with last year. From him from her from whom from where, and at its mythic origin she imagined a sailor bending a girl backward over coils of wet rope while behind them beat the dark sea.

She did not blame anyone, was simply trying to understand. For here was the terrible truth Harold had taught her: things did not happen, things were not real, it was the meaning behind them that was real. Therefore it all had significance. If she could just make it out. She tried to read the events of her life like a language, but only caught a phrase here and there. Yet she knew the meaning would eventually appear like invisible ink, a message inscribed on her body (as in the story Harold had read her), a message inscribed over and over until the body knew. She could almost feel the words rising from her flesh to her lips.

Late that afternoon she got up to go to the bathroom. Nothing came out, so she lay back down, and right away she had to go again. Still there was nothing, but when she stood she felt a twinge, sat, and what seemed several quarts of liquid and solid shot out of her all at once. She felt better. She cleaned herself and got back in bed. It was just nerves. She felt infinitely better. Cool. A tom-tom beat twice somewhere in her plumbing. The organs were settling back in place. If she could stay on top of this it would be all right. It beat again. A bubble floated toward her anus; she stopped it, moved it away and let it burst. A new one formed. Please, she thought.

Dinner arrived, and at the sight of the meat she raced to the toilet. A boiling porridge scalded her rectum, and between her legs she watched crimson serpents coil through the murky water. At the next explosion she shrieked. The lips of her anus sputtered like an idiot's, and as she became feverish she blamed herself for what was happening. It was her fault, she thought. She could have controlled it if she'd been more attentive. It was just will, Harold always said, pretend you aren't sick, and you won't be. But you had to keep on top of it every second, she had let it slip, and now . . .

When she was next conscious, she found a flexible, plastic tube coming through her abdominal wall and emptying into a transparent bag. She asked about this and was told she had perforated a bowel. Bacteria had eaten through the intestine, opening up communication between fecal matter and the bloodstream; this had triggered an attack of peritonitis, and they had decided to close off the entire system.

"How?" she asked.

They put it simply: her colon had been surgically cut, the downstream end sewn shut, the upstream end attached to a tube which was now slowly filling the plastic bag with a caramel liquid. It was a temporary measure. As soon as she was better . . . She understood without asking that she was not going home. Recovery now receded before her, retreated in step with her advance.

"What do they say?" I asked her.

"The infection is tenacious." It was a phrase she'd heard

them use. She was neither depressed nor pessimistic. Her insides were outside. "Kerner says I have bad protoplasm."

"What's that mean?"

She shook her head. She saw that I was worried and smiled to reassure me.

I said, "I'd like to talk to Kerner."

"He was here before."

I walked up the corridor to the nursing station. A male nurse sat there alone reading a novel. "The doctor is gone for the night."

"How can I reach him."

"If you call in the morning. Anytime after eight."

"Do you have a home number?"

"Are you a relative of the patient?"

"Come on, what's the—?"

"I'm sorry, we're not permitted to give it out."

"Okay, fine." I snatched up a phone book. "His name's John. Does he live in the city?" I flipped through the *K*'s. "John Kerner, M.D. . . . Here we go, on Clayton."

"Mr. Raab?" It was the head floor nurse this time. "Could I speak to you a minute?" I put down the book. "Dr. Kerner can't see anyone tonight, but if you leave your name, I'll be sure he contacts you tomorrow."

April 24

Tonight as I was eating dinner there was a knock, and before I had answered I knew who it would be. Lucy strolled in, perched on the window sill and surveyed the room. She said, "Harold, this place is awful."

I looked around. It seemed all right to me. "How did you find me?"

"Jimmy saw you on the street one day and followed you home. Do you mind that I came?"

I wasn't sure. I closed the door and sat down. "How is Jimmy?"

"He's fine. He's moving to Los Angeles in a couple of weeks. He got a job down there."

"Moving, huh." I felt a twinge, as if someone had pulled a plug, and a tepid bath had begun to drain. "I hadn't heard."

"How would you have heard?" said Lucy.

"That's true."

"Anyway, I didn't come to talk about that. Are you all right here?" She asked it like a friend who doesn't want to pry, but feels a responsibility.

"Pretty good. It was strange for a while, but now it's okay."

"Is it all right if I tell your parents? They've been on the phone to me."

"I'll call them."

"No, you won't." Lucy was tired, and her face stretched as if to crack and slough off a mask of fatigue that hardened there the moment she relaxed.

I said, "What's bad protoplasm?"

She smiled, "Did Kerner say that?"

"Apparently. Who is Kerner, Lucy?"

"The chief gynecology resident. She couldn't do better."

"He's the one you've been seeing?"

She shrugged, nodded. "Sometimes."

"Married guy, I hear."

"Yeah, but it's all right, Harold," she said, "his wife knows what's going on. We talk about it."

"You and the wife?"

"Me and the wife."

"God, how modern our little Lucille has gotten."

"I wouldn't say that."

"Just gone native, huh?"

She laughed. "Look who's talking." Fatigue had settled over her again without her noticing. Lucy was only twenty-seven, but already her hair was full of gray, and lines like fine wires were appearing around her eyes. She had grown drier, lately, crisper, and I could see time ticking in her skin, one two three four, like that, time taking her apart as if just the other day, last week perhaps, she'd suddenly been released from the eternity of youth.

"Bad protoplasm is a joke," Lucy said. "It means Kerner doesn't know why she isn't getting better."

"But she isn't?"

She shook her head. "For a couple of days she improves, then she slips. She perforates a bowel, loses weight, she won't eat. . . . None of it's that serious, it's the pattern. Because the more problems she has, the more they cause, and somewhere down the line we're going to get pneumonia or a renal failure. . . ."

All my life I have felt something coming. I have heard the wheels and seen the smoke, and as a child I would lie awake at night listening to it come, bringing consequences I was not prepared to consider. Yet it had always been so far off in the future that I did not have to think about it just yet, not just yet, but could instead drift off to sleep to the steady sound of the wheels. Then out on the pier with Mickey Marcus the other day, I looked up, and it was here.

I said, "What can I do?"

"Well, for one thing, visiting her in the middle of the night doesn't help. She stays up to see you when she should be sleeping."

"I didn't want to run into people."

"Poor baby . . ."

"All right, all right. What else?"

228

She thought a minute. Shook her head. "Nothing else."

"I feel like she needs—"

"You know what she needs?"

"What?"

"For you to relax. I need it, too, as a matter of fact. Why don't we have a drink."

"I haven't got anything."

"Then let's go out. I'll take you to the White Horse. Can you dance?"

"What do I have to do? You stand up there and bounce it around."

"Unh unh, they don't do that anymore."

"Since when?"

"They've got steps now."

"Steps?"

"Like this." She got off the window sill and, humming her own accompaniment, shuffled up and down the room with some tricky footwork. Even the hands moved to a plan.

"Are you kidding? I'm not doing that."

"Come on, it's easy." She did it slowly so I could follow. "You just go back, forward, step over, forward, back, then repeat. Try it."

"Who do you think you are, Zorba the Greek?"

"Uptight, sweetheart?"

"A little."

"You need a drink. Let's go to the White Horse."

"I don't have any money."

"It's okay, I'm loaded. Come on."

May 1

I have forgotten to mention that I got the job in the sandwich shop. I wash dishes and bus tables from eleven to three-thirty five days a week, two eighty an hour. It is mindless work, and I like it. I kid around with the other employees and complain about the boss like a normal person.

After work I go to the hospital and stay through dinner, usually until about eight or nine. I see everyone who comes to the room, Lucy, Kerner, Charlotte's mother, Joshua, Stephen (the erotic artist), Garth . . . Charlotte's mother sniffed at me like a suspicious dog (she must know something) and now is barely polite, but Joshua acted at once like I was an old friend who'd ridden the same range he had. We even compare notes on Charlotte, sometimes, Joshua asking, for instance, if it ever infuriated me how she expected things to be taken care of for her. Actually, I hadn't even noticed that, but I told him, "Yeah, it pissed me off all the time," and we laughed together.

Late one afternoon last week Charlotte was asleep, and I was sitting beside the bed reading the newspaper. No one else was in the room. I heard the door open behind me, a woman said, "Hi." I turned, and it was Donna standing there with Shaw. In the first instant I knew there was something between them, and I knew whose voice I'd heard from Shaw's window the night I took the Dodge.

Donna kissed me on the mouth and held me like I'd come back from the dead, and Shaw and I could barely look at each other. I felt that if I started crying then I would never stop. Shaw indicated the bed, "What's going on here?"

Charlotte had awakened and was smiling in surprise at the

visit. They stayed for half an hour, and it was strangely comfortable, Charlotte showing none of her usual self-consciousness around Shaw. She even teased him a little, no small trick, and entertained us with hospital horror stories. During the conversation Donna sat on the radiator behind Shaw's chair and rested a hand on his shoulder. He wasn't exactly at home with that, but he left it there.

When I saw them out to the elevator, I indicated the two of them as casually as possible and said, "So . . ."

Shaw just nodded.

Donna laughed out loud at this, then said to me, "If you need a place, we got a room no one's using."

I smiled. "I like it being empty."

May 25

I see that it has been almost a month since I wrote last, and it is going to be difficult to summarize what has happened in the meantime. I must say that I have grown weary of living my life twice, once out there in the world and a second time in this notebook. Yet when I think about stopping I remember a conversation I had with Charlotte a few weeks ago when she was still fairly alert. It was late, and as I was about to go home for the night she asked what I was doing with myself these days.

I said, "Nothing much. The usual."

She said, "Are you writing?"

"Sure. What else?"

"Finished anything?"

Ah. "What do you mean by that?"

"I don't know." She smiled. "You don't finish things, do you?"

She had a point. I have a problem with endings. Well, I will finish this.

For a long time after she perforated the bowel, Charlotte just hurt. The doctors asked where, and she wasn't sure. At first it was in her calf where she had phlebitis, then it moved to her lungs, her ribs, her kidney. Yet over the hours the pain paused in its wanderings ever longer in the lower region of her groin until it seemed that a fire had been or was still burning there; "had been or was still" because time had so distorted that she no longer knew if what she experienced were occurring in the present or had happened long ago and were being remembered.

"Is it Monday?" she asked the nurse.

"Tuesday, dear."

"Which Tuesday?"

Where was the present? She hypothesized such a place marked by calendars and clocks, yet she found that her sense of a present presumed an ability to fix on things in the immediate vicinity. An object trembling, as objects do, in the light that shimmers, as the light will, invented the present. But unable to get such a fix, everything perceived through a murky liquid, it all became a soup which, stirred with a circular movement, threw to the surface first this object, then that, in no particular order.

The days turned gray and the people with them. Sometimes they spoke, Charlotte answered, then they faded again, participated unwittingly in skeins of dreams, stepped in and out of her fantastical elaborations to go about their business.

Someone said, "You'll be all right now."

She realized with a thump of fear (a door opening, another closing), that the words "all right" were being used in a new and limited way. Things had happened that foreclosed the possibility of her ever being really right again. The key to the body was that you had a grip on it. She had not realized this until her grip began to loosen. Then she saw that her hand was weak, the thing itself was slippery.

Early in May Lucy found a lump in Charlotte's abdomen, called Kerner, and he agreed that it was the liver.

"Is that bad?" Charlotte asked.

"It isn't pie for dessert," Kerner said, "but it's not really a surprise."

They worried about her weight, and the nurse would sit with a spoonful of pudding poised at Charlotte's lips. But now that Charlotte understood she was "not doing well," she took it personally, became defiant, tried to show them she was strong, or at least courageous. Yet it was only the trying they saw.

The nurse said, "One more bite, dear."

"No, get that shit away from me."

"Just one."

She grew irritable. One morning she blew up at her mother, threw her out of the room, sent her back to Los Angeles. She wouldn't let her brother fly in from Houston. She refused visits from friends, hospital volunteers, social workers and a rabbi who'd come thinking Mrs. Cobin must be a Jew. Hadn't she converted? She smiled. What if they had children? She laughed. The rabbi was an older man, and after he'd gone she cried over the way she'd treated him.

One evening she asked me, "Where's Joshua?"

I started to answer, then realized it wasn't really a question. He had more or less disappeared lately, would pop in once or twice a day, read the chart, attempt a professional inspection of the patient, then frown at his watch and leave.

I said, "I think he's got the medicine clerkship. That takes up a lot of—"

"He did medicine last year," Charlotte said, "he's on a research elective now." She smiled.

I managed to track Joshua down a couple hours later in the cafeteria. He was having coffee with a pretty woman in a white coat, and when he saw me he looked guilty as hell. The woman noticed this and excused herself. I said, "You want to get a drink?"

We went to a bar and drank. Neither of us even mentioned Charlotte for a couple of rounds, just shot the irrelevant breeze until out of nowhere Joshua said, "Listen, I've got to tell you something . . ." He looked to see what I was going to think of this. "I've been thinking a lot about divorcing her once she's better."

I said, "Yeah, well . . ." and gestured that I wasn't too surprised.

"I mean you couldn't put up with her either."

"Oh, now, wait a second, that was completely different, that was between her and me. The two of you . . . I know how you felt about her Joshua."

He glanced at me, wondering what secrets I'd been told, then shook his head. "It only looked that way."

"Don't give me that," I said, "I remember when you met her."

"What are you talking about? You didn't even know us then."

"You were this big, handsome, uptight stud, and all the girls were hot for you. But you were scared, so you went out with Charlotte because you thought you might not have to fuck her right away. She made picnic lunches and took you on these dumb walks in the woods, and you fooled around, and you fooled around, and finally you kind of slipped into it going backwards, right?"

He smiled.

"And you lay in the grass looking at the clouds like you hadn't done since you were ten. You thought, why did I stop looking at the clouds?"

Joshua said nothing, only watched as a third tequila sunrise rose over the dregs of the second, and he was given a new napkin.

I said, "You gave that up. Not her."

"Maybe I just missed her too much, and it snapped."

"If you spent a little more time with her . . . Whatever happens later, that'd help now."

"No, sure, I know. When I saw you in the cafeteria tonight, I thought, Oh, shit. . . . Plus I was embarrassed, you seeing me with Becky."

"Please," I said, "I'd do the same thing if I were you."

The infection persisted in Charlotte's liver. Drugs contained its advance, but where it passed it left scar tissue, and this closed off the hepatic channels just as gonorrhea scarring had twisted her fallopian tube. One morning Lucy asked John Kerner about the prognosis.

"We'll move her upstairs, Monday," he said.

"Really?" said Lucy. "Upstairs? She's better?"

"We're just dealing with the liver now. That's a slow process. There isn't a legitimate need for intensive care at this point."

"She's not doing well, is she, John?"

"Not brilliantly, but she's been to war. Give her time."

In time the contracting channels impeded intestinal blood on its passage through the liver. Fluid seeped into her abdomen which swelled, blocking the diaphragm and making breathing difficult. The fluid was drained. Five days later it had refilled and had to be drained again. Then her legs swelled.

She grew erratically worse. She ate the pudding without complaint. She stopped talking about the gallery job which, presumably, had been filled by someone else. She stopped complaining about Joshua or the nurse, and she did not make plans for getting better. There was only pain, only the moment.

My own life by this time seemed hardly to exist. I went to work, to the hospital, came back to my room and slept. As I saw that Charlotte was not going to get well on her own, I became increasingly preoccupied with designs for luring her back to health. I had made her fall in love with me, made her leave her husband; I had made her happy, made her come, made her cry. At times it seemed I made her up out of whole cloth, so what should stop me from making her well as well?

So I dangled pleasures (sex, drugs, gluttony). I contrived little dramas to make it seem Joshua was seeing other women. No one knows death well enough to fear it, but I tried to frighten her with those death-enlarged versions of what we fear all our lives: pain, abandonment, the loss of self-control. Anything to shake that unearthly detachment and make the outcome of the next minute of some interest and concern.

None of it worked. She had finally seen that I was playing games and with that went all my power. That is what infuriates us about the dying; they resist us utterly, and we see that we are dying, too, relative to them.

When all of this had failed, when her face showed nothing but a vague regret at having disappointed me, I stopped trying. I continued to visit her, but it had become a ritual instead of an act.

I grew calmer. Life had changed. I still had bad moments; one day at work I saw a trash basket filled with broken glass and was seized with an impulse to plunge my arm in up to the elbow. But this was really not such an odd thought, and the fact that I didn't, that I was called to shred lettuce and by the next time I looked the basket had been emptied, all reassured me.

As I read over the pages I have written this morning I am struck by their strange tranquility. This is largely an effect of telling everything from a distance, and in one way that is a blessing; it will be relatively short. But it is also inaccurate, concealing not only numerous events, but the central feature of this experience: the passage and accumulation and eroding effects of time. It is time I cannot reproduce here, that I cannot even remember. Instead I give details like Charlotte falling asleep while I tried to masturbate her, or a letter from her mother in which a *d* was substituted for an *r* at the end of the first word so that the greeting read: "Dead Charlotte . . ." And these are nothing, touches, not the thing touched.

It was during this time that Jimmy Wax moved to Los Angeles. The day before he left, he took Shaw and me to lunch. We spent a long, cheerful afternoon drinking wine and reminiscing over what was about to become our past. Jimmy had changed already: a handsome vest, new shoes, hair and beard neatly trimmed. He had an apartment in Santa Monica, a job waiting; just a gofer to start, but who knew where from there, gaffer, grip, and when they found out how good he was (but was he?) cutting A and B roles, assistant editor . . . there was sky at the top, the room was the limit.

Shaw and I listened in silence. If we had accused him of going to Hollywood, we would have also had to admit that he was going to Hollywood. We felt superior and intimidated; Jimmy was embarrassed and proud.

"We'll all be down there together some day," Jimmy said.

"We might all be down there," said Shaw, "but it won't be together."

"Why not?"

Shaw shrugged, yet it was clearly true. "This was just a phase."

"So is everything," said Jimmy Wax.

Then he was gone, and Shaw and I sat there alone. In a minute one of us would leave, then the other, and only the table would remain, a glimmer of light on its varnished surface. It hurt to lose Jimmy, but to lose Shaw was a positive grief.

Finally he asked me, "How is she?"

And when I said, "Dying," it was the first time I'd admitted it to myself.

A week later it seemed everyone knew. One dreary evening Mickey Marcus appeared at the hospital and asked if it would be all right for him to "talk to Charlotte about it" for a while. It. I tried not to understand, but Mickey was persistent, he wet his lips to explain. "I'm really looking into the whole thanatology area, and I thought . . . I understand the delicacy . . ."

I said, "Who's this for?"

"The *Stone,* but it's going to be good, Harold. It's going to be serious."

And who could blame him? We were all just as fascinated, for it was presumed that Charlotte had been granted insights and initiated into mysteries inaccessible to the rest of us. Death was more glamorous even than madness. People wanted to talk to her, sit in her presence, exchange their compassion for a glimpse of eternity through eyes that saw. She was the first who would ever burst (at least among us) into that silent sea, and therefore her dying became a part of all of ours. Once the ice was broken, anyone could fall through. And we wanted death to exist for us. It would harden the focus of our lives and invest each detail with the throb of its opposite, the throb that made things shimmer and pulse.

But in the end I had to deny Mickey his interview. The sad fact was that Charlotte, herself, did not yet officially "know." Rather, her flesh knew, but it had not quite informed the mind, and Mickey Marcus did not seem the proper messenger of that news.

Then how did Charlotte finally learn? It began one morning when she was feeling pretty good. The nurse came in and asked how she was, so she put on a smile and said, "Pretty good. I think I'll go out in the lounge later on."

The nurse said, "All right, call me when you want to."

And that was not the reaction Charlotte had expected. Perfunctory. After weeks of immobility, here was this sign of extraordinary improvement, and the nurse acted as if she had said anything at all, had said nothing, as if she were dead. She began to watch the others: Joshua was too solicitous; Harold was unnaturally solemn; Kerner, she realized, did not distinguish between the living and the dead. Only Lucy failed to accuse her of death. Lucy had become so gentle that this didn't seem the same person at all, but a secret Lucy risen to the surface and displacing the original, like a fairy tale in which behind a mud door lay the starry kingdom.

The next day she took a mirror from the night table and looked at herself. Her skin was dead, her hair was dead, her teeth, her gums and the whites of her eyes were all turning brown. Hope, which had remained a shred, now tore through, and she fell twenty-one stories onto the pillow. She wished, as she dropped, that she might land in death, but at the bottom (a bottom that produced the nauseating effect of lifting her upward even as she continued to fall) she found that she had only begun.

"There is nothing we can do for her now," someone might have said.

Yet she was obliged to go on. And here a strange thing occurred: everything reversed. The task was no longer to summon the strength necessary to recover; it was to marshall the concentration and will needed to die. Now the weaker she became, the longer she would have to go on living in this condition. She struggled to reach the end, but the closer she got the slower she moved. Wasn't there a paradox in which an arrow never reached its target?

One evening she asked John Kerner, "How am I?"

"How do you feel?"

She replied with a look that devastated him, that despised him for not being straight with her.

"The liver isn't responding well," he said, "you know that."

She wouldn't give him the satisfaction.

"We're trying to control the scarring, but it's difficult."

"What if you can't?"

"The liver will eventually stop functioning."

"And then?"

"A person can't live without a liver."

She smiled. They were more afraid than she who was mostly curious. She considered the nature of the thing. Was it a different state into which one passed like at birth or puberty? Was it an absence, a sensation, a quadrant of a circle? Or was it this growing indifference she felt for everything carried to its logical limit? But notions of death were just notions, concepts within life; within death, she believed, there were no concepts.

She considered the end of her nose. Neither odor nor sensation passed through it, yet of all the parts of her body it was the most reliable. Whenever she lost her bearings she began to look for her nose, and around it the rest of the body would reassemble itself. And how comforting, orderly and even amusing it was that whenever she found it, it was invariably right where it had been the last time, search for it as she might in the farthest flung corners of the room.

She settled behind it now because she wanted to say something to Harold. He was the only person she could trust. She had said to Joshua, "Look, please . . ." and he had pretended not to understand. She had said, "Give me a shot of something."

"They're giving you everything they can."

"That's not what I mean."

She looked at the ceiling. She wanted to say, "Harold, this is awful. At a certain point . . ." She wanted to say, ". . . ." But how could words carry such thoughts?

She thought of girls in the schoolyard choosing sides for kickball and of the one girl who was left to last. She stood alone against the diamond mesh of the fence.

She had to speak once more and tell Harold what she had hesitated to say so far. She was ready, but the fever returned, and her mouth was no longer within her domain. Snakes slid through her head. Now he would have to understand without being told; he would have to learn for himself what an atrocity this was.

Late last night I was awakened by a pounding on my door, and when I opened it, Roger was standing there naked telling me, "There's some crazy bitch on the phone says she has to talk to you."

By the time I got to the hospital, Lucy was already there. Charlotte was in tears saying, "This is awful. Lucy, please . . ."

"Please what?" said Lucy. She was still groggy with sleep. "Is there pain?"

Charlotte shook her head in frustration.

"Then what?"

Charlotte wept.

I knew what. I said, "Lucy . . ."

She said, "Shut up, she needs a sedative."

"No," it was Charlotte saying, "no," and extending a hand that hardly had the strength to hold itself up. The room emptied of discussion. Charlotte said, "Lucy, I'm miserable."

Lucy said, "I know."

"I can't stand it anymore."

"I know."

"I've been here for months. I'm not getting better. There's nothing you can do for me." In a professional reflex Lucy began to disagree, but Charlotte interrupted screaming, "There isn't anything," screaming, "there isn't . . ." until the very frailty of her voice seemed to amplify it and silence Lucy. She looked at me for the first time. "Do you see, Harold?"

Unavoidably I did. A cord ran from the wall socket to a cardiac pacemaker. An intravenous tube fed her Aramine to keep the blood pressure up. The paths of these cables, the casual loops into which the flexible tubing fell became sinister and demanding. There was no way to deal with them. I closed my eyes, but they persisted. They are still there now.

———————

May 27

I went back to the house this morning. On the bench just inside the door were a stack of political science library books, some junk mail and a letter from my father. I folded this in half and put it in my pocket. Upstairs Donna and Shaw were half awake in Shaw's bed. I said, "You two look pretty together."

They got up, and while we ate breakfast, I described the scene at the hospital. At the end Shaw asked what else Charlotte had said. I shook my head. "That was all. She never said it explicitly."

Donna said, "Said what explicitly?"

Shaw said, "It sounds like that's what she meant."

"There's no doubt in my mind." I turned to Donna. "Said explicitly she wants to die."

"Die?" She looked from me to Shaw, trying to assess if this were just another bad joke.

"Maybe we could put out a contract on her," said Shaw, "send a couple of guys in sunglasses up there . . ."

"Or we could chuck her out the window and say she jumped."

"Anyway," said Donna, "who says it's hopeless? Does Lucy?"

"What does Lucy say?" Shaw asked.

"Not a lot. Doctors seem reluctant to acknowledge these things."

"Then how can you?"

Shaw said, "Let me ask you, Donna, do you think there are ever times when people ought to consider—"

"Maybe sometimes, but—"

"And if the doctors won't, who's going to?"

"Not you."

"All right, fine, not me. Who?"

"Wait a minute, man . . ." This was not how she wanted the conversation to go. ". . . The woman is a fucking human being."

"Yeah, maybe we ought to think about that," said Shaw, "because pretty soon she's just going to be the fleshy end of a machine."

I laughed.

Donna just looked at Shaw, and he looked back, but no one can compete with him at that game, so finally she got up and cleared the table.

He knew this was precisely what drove her crazy about him, the coldness, she called it, and he said nothing to correct the misconception. Shaw liked being taken for a bastard, and Donna's contempt, like coffee grounds in this silence, pleased him. This was his style, cold coffee (he drank his) and butts (he lit one from the ashtray), a hole in the sleeve of his sweater, another in the toe of his boot, and his exquisite lips curling like a painted river in a smile of sensuality that was not; not the usual, anyway.

Donna brought a pot of fresh coffee to the table, filled our cups and carried hers out to the piano where she began to play.

"One way to go," said Shaw, "is to find out what narcotics she's on and see if we can get a lot of them somewhere."

I nodded.

"Meanwhile, try to learn how you can disrupt the life-support apparatus. What do they call that?"

"Pulling the plug."

"Right. Get to know the relevant plugs."

People always said of Shaw that he was the hardest, the farthest, the last one; that he was out there, down there, from there. The offerings others made, he declined to burn. He bore no false sentiment, paid no deference, his doubt benefited no one, his heart softened not, neither did it yield, and he shed his tears equally on all, which was to say, none on any. Yet by virtue of this rigor he permitted himself the single vanity that if the earth bore a single human slightly less sanctimonious than the rest, one whose percentage of hypocrisy fell at all below a hundred, perhaps it was he. So despite (or because of) the strictures he applied to himself, the austerity of form and consequent sparseness of content, there was no truer heart than Shaw's and no warmer love, cold as it might be.

"Just remember," he said, "if you don't do this, no one's going to."

"You think?"

"Believe me. Joshua can't, he isn't a killer. Lucy's a killer, but she doesn't care enough to risk it. Now you," he said, "you're a killer and you care, but your problem, Harold, is you always mistake the killer in you for a lack of caring. Then you might not do it just to prove you aren't a bastard, whereas the fact is it'll prove just the opposite."

May 28

Lucy says, "Don't think about it. Do not even say the words."

29

It isn't that simple. If Charlotte would die all at once, we could endure it. There might even be a moment of illumination and things revealed. But death works by the piece, not the job. Already the face does not belong to her. Disease has so ravaged it that over the weeks her expression, the cast of her features has yielded, line by line, that complex facial language, the casuistry of sighs and smiles by which it had always communicated the things Charlotte felt and wanted to feel and wanted. It is nearly blank now, as if out near the frontier of death there might finally be a place beyond vanity and deceit.

30

This evening Lucy and I were there alone watching. There was very little left to see. From time to time she shifted her weight or moved an arm. After an hour she woke, and it was difficult to tell if she recognized us, but she managed to ask, "What time is it?"

I laughed, and Charlotte grinned, pleased to have told a joke. Lucy said that it was twenty to seven.

She looked at the window. "But there's still some light."

"We're on daylight savings, now."

"Is it summer already?"

"Almost."

She nodded. "Good."

A moment later she was asleep again. Lucy continued to stare at the bed as if not permitting herself to look away. I said, "At least we should talk to Joshua and see what he thinks."

She said nothing.

"I'll call him."

———————————

June 1

"Liver deaths are slow," Lucy was saying. "Pneumonia might finish it in a few hours, but more likely we'll have to wait for the liver. When I talked to Kerner this morning, he thought she might last another month."

Joshua looked up, "Another month?"

"She's signed the form authorizing that no extraordinary measures be—"

"I know that."

"Did you see her tonight?"

"Just for a minute." He had been disappearing again lately, but even in a minute he would have understood why we had called him. Charlotte had been stretched out on the bed, a puddle of flesh from which issued a low, irregular moaning. Tremors, spasms and waves of fever passed over the body like wind. Bedsores spread out in raspberry continents; the flesh cracked, broke, stank. The hour of the machine had come.

"The question," said Lucy, "is what we want to do about it."

He nodded.

She said, "Do you want to do it?"

He went on nodding, though this apparently meant nothing for a moment later he said, "Do it?" as though he had just understood what we were talking about. Through the windows behind him, the tips of the enormous arbor vitae touched a gasoline sky. I sat on the arm of the chair in which he'd put Charlotte that first night when her ankle gave out. He was on the same footstool. Somehow we had come back to where we'd started except that Charlotte was missing. He said to me, "You'd do it, wouldn't you? In my place."

He didn't know the extent to which I was in his place, but I didn't mention it. I had called him only to get the ball rolling in Lucy's mind and because it seemed he had the right to first refusal. Yet even if he said yes, I knew we could never count on Joshua, so the most merciful thing was to discourage him. "I don't know," I said, "in your position I'm not sure a person could."

* * *

He went home to think it over, and I came here. It is four in the morning. I haven't slept, but sat beside the bed thinking she might die as I watched. In every breath there is a hesitation, a little death between the exhale and the inhale, and I can almost touch it there in the stillness. Yet just as I think it is finally over, she starts the other way and goes on.

---

7 A.M.

Shit. Half an hour ago she had some respiratory problem and instead of thinking I panicked and called the nurse. An intern was hustled up from surgery, he cut a hole in her throat, and now they've got a tube running from there to a gray machine that says Honeywell. The machine pumps air, and Charlotte's chest rises and falls like a piece of pneumatic equipment.

Therefore the rest of this is my responsibility. It must be done without fear or uncertainty. It must be so simple that I hardly notice. No thought. Nothing else. Just do it. And if I am caught, if there are consequences, fine. I have no shame.

10:30 A.M.

Lucy was just here. She had had breakfast with Joshua, and he'd told her he wasn't going to do it. He'd given a curious reason. "It's Charlotte's death. I can't take it from her." Lucy had assured him Charlotte didn't want it, but Joshua would not be moved.

"Then it's just us," I said.

She nodded.

"How do we do it?"

"And not get caught?" She thought a minute. "Potassium chloride, probably. Inject it into the IV and she'd go into fibrillations within five minutes. On intensive care we'd have a cardiac monitor to worry about, but with her up here now . . ."

"What if they do an autopsy?"

"She's dehydrated so you'd expect an elevated potassium level. Anyway, they wouldn't do one on a case like this."

"Then it doesn't much matter what we use."

"Just something quick and clean."

"When?"

"Tonight at six. There's a lull right after they serve dinner. That's the safest time."

"All right, I'll wait for you here."

———

12:15

When she is dead . . .

Two o'clock.

For Joshua, killing Charlotte is impossible; at once too monumental and too insignificant. For me it is just the right size. It will hurt, but only a little. I am not losing a part of myself. If that sounds callous, it is also necessary, for who could go this far with her unless he were detached? And it is interesting that the great cruelty of the past, my refusal to give Charlotte love, now becomes itself the gift.

It's just like they say, once one accepts his horror, it ceases to be that.

Three. Activity. Nurses, doctors, tests, writing on the chart, a new glucose bottle, fresh sheets, a sponge bath . . . Then it all vanishes, and Charlotte and I are alone again, preparing for death. She is preparing, and I am preparing, and the only sound is the steady beat of the respirator.

Four, past four. I think of her vagina growing cold, and it is as though I will partake of her death through it, as though what I have left behind there will no longer be nourished. Strange, but it's pleasant to think of dying like that, the fractional death we suffer when those who possess part of us die themselves. One is spread about in cunts and mouths, in hearts and hands and thoughts, one is here and there, one is not himself, one is not just one. That is the absurdity of rented rooms.

Shaw is right. I can kill. In my heart it is done already.

Has it changed me? Only in that one becomes more and more himself, which is to say more and more a stranger until finally he is not a person at all anymore, but himself. Then he is no longer bound by the strictures of humanity, and strangeness itself becomes the guide instead. That is the way we all go.

Five. An hour. The dinner trays will be here soon. I will recognize the sound of the stainless steel carts rolling off the elevator. By quarter to six everyone will be served.

Did I ever love her, even once, even for a moment? I don't know. Perhaps love is beyond me. I seem to see it out there in the dim distance, yet when I think of her death I feel nothing. Or if not nothing, only a vague sadness that seems to have little to do with Charlotte. Sadness is the bedrock, isn't it, that bolt of feeling beneath everything.

It is an afternoon in the fall of 1953. A boy of eight is walking home from school. Above the athletic fields to his right, the sky is dark with an approaching storm front. The boy is sad, but not unhappy. He does not distinguish between the bank of clouds and the swell of emotion in his heart. He feels himself possessed of an enormous power. Of all the events of his life, these are among the few he never considers telling to anyone. Later he will try to name them, and in the very effort lose his sure sense of what they are.

From the window I watch cars moving on the wet street and houses running down the hill to the sea. The houses are white, the water black, the sky a neutral gray. The rain has stopped. There are the carts. It is ten to six.

I think of her vagina growing cold and of her heart. I think of a world from which Charlotte is absent. I think of the rest

251

of us following her, one by one, and of a field out behind a barn on an afternoon in August when all of us are dead. I think of the years between now and then that will be our lives, and they seem over already.

So perhaps we die together after all, Charlotte and I, a little bit, a little bit. I was wrong, I do lose a part of myself. I would not mind losing some more.

A nurse sticks her head in and smiles. Pretty cute. It is five past.

―――――――

June 2

At ten past six the room phone rang, and it was Lucy telling me to come to her apartment.

I said, "Shaw sure had this one figured."

She didn't say anything.

"What's the story?"

"I'll tell you when you get here."

But suddenly I did not really care. Lucy would have her reasons, but they would only be reasons. I said, "Okay, I'll be there in a minute," and hung up.

I did not move right away, but sat with my hand on the receiver looking off in the direction I was already facing: a bit of window, the bank of outlets below the sill, a section of wall, of linoleum floor, my foot . . . The room was silent, empty.

I looked at her chest. A fold appeared in the hospital gown right at the breastbone, deepened slightly then grew shallow. She was still at work. Just a bit more, she must have been thinking, then a bit beyond that.

* * *

Within each second she drifted and returned. Death slipped from her grip just as life had, and she felt she would never get there, but hang suspended like a leaf in amber. Someone was here beside her, trying to help, but she had no time for that. She inched toward dying, trying to relax involuntary muscles and get them to release things they spasmodically grasped. It was like learning to come, but harder. Letting go of even the smallest fragment (an effort requiring all her concentration) was nevertheless far easier than keeping herself from seizing it again a moment later in a reflex of fear.

Her extremities, of course, had long been superfluous. They lay at the edge of the universe. But the center, the seat of disease, was warm and lit with a strange dark light. Her task was to get into the light, into the glowing filament. Several times she came close, but at the last minute would be distracted, reach out and grab this thing as it was going past and cling to it with a fond longing. She still lacked the ability to finish. It was no longer a matter of strength or will, only of technique. Like a dance, like coming, like everything, you needed the knack.

When the final pass came, she knew this one was different. There was fear, but even that had become an object. She nodded to it and went on. She felt her life beat irregularly like something about to give out, felt it hesitate, halt, get going again. This was the last thing she would have to let go, and the irony was that she had worked so long at dying that her body did not know how to quit. The final obstacle was her own effort, which, having brought her this far, kept her from going the rest of the way.

Time no longer existed, only this perpetual instant, across which she made her way alone. Toward what? Not the other side (there were no sides), not a figure, not release. These were only concepts within life; within death . . . Death was nothing, she finally realized. She thought of telling them, but they would not understand what she meant, and she wouldn't understand either. Yet it was easy after all, and she saw that all her magnificent effort had been unnecessary. She could have done nothing, and it would have happened anyway. Too bad they didn't know. She felt a detached sympathy for their ignorance, but who were they? They were actually she who had never known this. There seemed even a form of her back there not knowing it still, but there was no communicating with that person.

She looked at that poor girl who lacked a nose. Where was her nose? She watched her search for it in all the corners of the room, but she couldn't find it, nor was it on her face where it had always been. She realized that at long last she had no nose. It was gone. And she followed it.

The respirator was an automatically initiated model. With it unplugged, Charlotte could not get any air through the closed rubber valves. Her chest flexed with the effort.

After a minute her body shuddered, the eyes opened and looked at me. It was an engaging look, frank and direct. It asked nothing and offered nothing in return, simply held me a moment, then went straight through and out the other side as if I were not there. And though by then I could not endure the sight, I could not look away either. Do you want it, it, the irreducible nub of things? Well, here it is.

With two fingers I closed the lids. I plugged the machine back in, Charlotte's chest rose and fell again, and fluid continued to drain into the arm.

An orderly pushed open the door and set it with a rubber stop. He collected all the towels from the bathroom and threw them into a wheeled basket in the corridor. Then he noticed me and came over to the bed. "How's the chick?" I shrugged. He nodded sagely, and we stood watching her a moment, then left the room together.

I went down the fire stairs and out of the hospital. I couldn't remember where I'd left my car, so I started out on foot toward Lucy's apartment. It was dusk. Lights had gone on in all the buildings giving them the velvet look of that hour. I thought: finally the night. I could not feel my feet or the air on my skin. I did not hear the sounds of the street.

At an intersection ahead of me a bus was stopped for a red light. For some reason I thought it was my bus, and I began to run toward it. The light turned green. I ran harder, calling and waving my arms, but by the time I reached the corner there were just two taillights moving off up the hill. I stood on the street in the clouds of white exhaust it had left behind. These swirled around me a moment, then slowly rose, separating into bays and lakes, into rivers, straits and slender streams through whose semitransparence the moon shone ever brighter until the exhaust stretched itself beyond thinness and vanished altogether into the night.

There was more, of course, but that will do for now.

Home delivery from Pocket Books

Here's your opportunity to have fabulous bestsellers delivered right to you. Our free catalog is filled to the brim with the newest titles plus the finest in mysteries, science fiction, westerns, cookbooks, romances, biographies, health, psychology, humor—every subject under the sun. Order this today and a world of pleasure will arrive at your door.

POCKET BOOKS, Department ORD
1230 Avenue of the Americas, New York, N.Y. 10020

Please send me a free Pocket Books catalog for home delivery

NAME _____

ADDRESS _____

CITY _____ STATE/ZIP _____

If you have friends who would like to order books at home, we'll send them a catalog too—

NAME _____

ADDRESS _____

CITY _____ STATE/ZIP _____

NAME _____

ADDRESS _____

CITY _____ STATE/ZIP _____

368